Out of Body

ALSO BY JEFFREY FORD

Vanitas

The Physiognomy

Memoranda

The Beyond

The Fantasy Writer's Assistant

The Portrait of Mrs. Charbuque

The Empire of Ice Cream

The Girl in the Glass

The Cosmology of the Wider World

The Drowned Life

The Shadow Year

Crackpot Palace

A Natural History of Hell

The Twilight Pariah

Ahab's Return

The Best of Jeffrey Ford

OUT OF
BODY

JEFFREY FORD

A TOM DOHERTY ASSOCIATES BOOK
NEW YORK

This is a work of fiction. All of the characters, organizations, and events portrayed in this novella are either products of the author's imagination or are used fictitiously.

OUT OF BODY

Copyright © 2020 by Jeffrey Ford

Cover photographs © Getty Images
Cover design by FORT

Edited by Ellen Datlow

A Tor.com Book
Published by Tom Doherty Associates
120 Broadway
New York, NY 10271

www.tor.com

Tor® is a registered trademark of
Macmillan Publishing Group, LLC.

ISBN 978-1-250-25014-8 (ebook)
ISBN 978-1-250-25015-5 (trade paperback)

First Edition: May 2020

For Ellen Datlow, good friend and editor
through all the years and pages

Out of Body

1

OWEN SAT WITH A cup of coffee at the kitchen table and stared out the glass door that offered a view of his tiny backyard. It was surrounded at its boundary by tall fir trees, and, at its center, there was a bird feeder hanging on a shepherd's crook, leaning easterly in the wind and wet mud. The sparrows swarmed what was left of the seed he'd put out two days earlier. While his visitors fluttered and pecked, his thoughts were of Sleeping Beauty, virulent thorns, and a turreted castle in the distance. She was dressed in azure robes, he noted, like the Virgin Mary, and her trailing golden hair had stars in it. In the background, there was a night sky with a crescent moon and stars of its own.

The scene Owen envisioned was painted on the wall of the children's section at the local library where he was and had been the head and only librarian for the past ten years. The painting, nearly as old as the one-story stucco building that held it, had seen better days. In the last five years the picture had become "ill," and it was said by those who tend to the upkeep of murals that the paint was in *structural peril*. He had a professional in to assess the damage, and the fellow told him what it would cost to restore it. Thousands more than the library budget. Its particular illness was a kind of paint separation that began with cracks and advanced into the curling away and dropping off of paint chips. Like a plague, the problem was spreading, creeping up Sleeping Beauty's neck toward her serene face.

He continuously pondered how he might raise the money but knew full well that in two years, his library on the back road, nestled at the edge of the forest next to the train tracks, would be closed. Five local, small-town libraries would be gathered into one larger one, sharing a budget and a new location. Owen's place had been built in 1948 and served the small suburban town since then. He went as a child and was enchanted by the mural above the children's books, as was his father. For the past twenty years the town had kept the library operating out of a sense of nostalgia more than anything else.

There were regular customers, mostly retirees, who came for books and to sit in the afternoon quiet and stare out the plate glass window on the adult side. It offered the view of a field of weeds, then a tree line of tall oaks, and, not quite obscured by the shadow of the forest, abandoned train tracks. In the evenings, in autumn, just before he'd lock up, deer would appear in the field.

The town of Westwend, on the edge of the pine barrens, moved at a radically slow pace.

This was about as far as he got in his calculations every morning while watching the birds. It was time to wash out his coffee cup and dress for work. That day it was the blue-gray suit, white shirt, no tie. The only alternative was the brown suit, white shirt, no tie. Locking the door behind him, he walked to the corner and turned left, making for town along a tree-lined sidewalk. The rain had stopped overnight but the wind was raging and the new leaves on the spring trees made a rushing noise like a rain-swollen creek.

If Owen was anything, he was a man of habit. At 7:05 every morning, he would arrive at the Busy Bee convenience store on the corner of Voss and Green. There, he always purchased a large coffee and a buttered roll. And as always, upon entering, he waved to Helen Roan, the owner's daughter, working behind the counter. She was just out of high school and saving money to attend a state college by the following fall. She had her sights set on being an English major. Owen admired the quixotic nature of her plan, its blatant impracticality, its vow of poverty. He'd known her since she was seven and first came to the library with her mother.

"How are your folks?" he asked on the way to the coffee station. He took one sugar, one dollop of half-and-half (he never used a stirrer but let it slosh together on the remainder of his walk).

"They're good. You know, my dad's living a life of quiet desperation; my mom, loud desperation."

Owen laughed. He was energized by her smile and intelligence.

Helen held the buttered roll wrapped in wax paper. As he headed toward her, she asked, "Cigarettes today?"

He shuddered. "Don't tempt me," he said. "I'm trying to lay off."

She put the roll on the counter and turned to the cash register. As it rang its tally, the bell on the front door also jingled. Someone entered the store and swept in between Helen and Owen. The interloper was dressed in a black jacket, pants, and boots, and nearly knocked the cup out of Owen's hand.

The librarian took a step back, absolutely fine with this customer being served before him. Owen never looked for a fight. He'd been in one in grade school and lost badly. Even a loud argument now was more than he cared to deal with. He heard Helen say, "Mister, you'll have to get in line. This customer was here before you."

"It's OK," said Owen. "I'm fine." And then something happened. He couldn't see what it was; he just saw the expression of sick surprise on Helen's face. Only when she backed away and put her hands out in front of her did

he see the stranger's arm come up and follow her movement. In his hand was a black revolver. Owen froze. He
heard the man say, "Open the register and give me the
money." It became immediately evident Helen was in a
similar state of paralysis.

"I'm not fucking around," said the man.

Owen meant to jump the gunman from behind, but
instead of his arms and legs moving, his mouth opened
slightly and a short, strangled cry escaped. In response,
the man swung his arm without turning completely
around and smashed the librarian in the jaw with the butt
of the gun. The attack came in a blur. The next Owen
knew, he was reeling backward into a stand of snacks, and
lights in his head were blinking. He staggered, tripped,
and fell to the floor, snacks flying in all directions, bags
popping beneath him. As he tumbled into darkness, he
heard a gunshot in the distance.

Owen came to in a panic, ringing in his ears. There
was a cop squatting next to him. "Easy, brother," said the
officer as he grabbed Owen's left arm. "Take a few deep
breaths."

He did as he was told, and the ringing slowly subsided.
Behind it was the percussion of his racing pulse. Things
beyond the immediate face of the cop revealed themselves slowly, and he watched, entranced, as reality put
the jigsaw of itself back together. He saw other officers

moving around. He sensed a crowd outside. In an instant he remembered what happened. "The girl behind the counter," he said to the cop.

There was an expression on the man's face as if weighing some decision. "Deceased," he finally said.

"No. You can't be right."

"I'm afraid it's true."

"What?"

"He shot her twice but not before she pushed the button letting us know there was a robbery. We got here when he was trying to get into the register. We put him down. You were out cold through the entire thing."

"Good lord," said Owen, and at first didn't realize there were tears streaming down his face. He wiped his eyes with the sleeve of his jacket.

"I'm gonna get a paramedic over here. Don't try to stand up. Don't move at all. We'll get you checked out and off to the hospital."

The paramedic turned out to be another kid Owen recognized from the library. He remembered first shaking hands with the boy beneath the scene of Sleeping Beauty years earlier, and recalled his name was Caleb. The young fellow took his blood pressure, shined a flashlight in his eyes, and performed a dozen other tests. Owen worked to collect himself. When the blue dots cleared from his eyes, he noticed the paramedic was trembling.

"Did you know Helen?" They were the same age and the town was so small.

Caleb didn't answer. Instead, bottom lip quivering and pale as an empty page, he said, "OK. Do you have any intense pain in your back or legs? How about chest or shoulders?"

"No."

"They're bringing in the stretcher."

A few minutes later, he was hoisted onto a bed with wheels. He requested that they put the head of the bed up, as he had a phobia about lying flat on his back. He'd suffered attacks of sleep paralysis in his early teens, and would freak out if he found himself in that position. After adjusting the bed, the second paramedic pumped the hydraulics of the conveyance, and Owen rose to see the scene clearly for the first time. He went lightheaded—yellow police tape, the bullet-riddled front window that should have shattered, six-packs of bottled soda stacked near the register for a quick sale, leaking from their wounds onto the linoleum.

They rolled him slowly toward the front door. The sunlight shining in made him squint and turn his head. When he did, he found he was facing the counter. Behind it he caught a glimpse of Helen—right eye, a burnt, bloody socket, left, glazed and staring, and a gaping flesh and blood blossom of a hole in her throat. Lying across her legs on his back was the gunman, none of his own wounds visible but a pool of blood beneath. Eyes closed, he appeared to simply be asleep, save for the froth on his lips and the fly on his forehead he wasn't swatting away. Just before being blocked from the horrible sight by the second paramedic, Owen noticed a small black tattoo of a circle with a cross inside it on the gunman's left wrist. At first, he'd thought it a second fly.

A group of ten people, which was a crowd in Westwend, stood outside the store, peering in. When Owen came out into the sunlight, they all applauded.

"They're cheering for you," said the second paramedic.

"Why?"

"You managed not to get killed," Caleb whispered.

2

OWEN WAS TAKEN TO a hospital three towns away and was thoroughly inspected. There were long periods of waiting, punctuated by brief visits with nurses who gave shots and took him for tests. He spent lonely hours, the TV on and meaning nothing, sunk in a depression as he contemplated the loss of Helen, what it would mean to her parents and the town. It was during one of these bouts of utter sadness that he wondered what might have happened had he jumped the gunman. But there wasn't a chance in hell he could ever have mustered the courage to do it. He'd nearly pissed his pants when he saw the gun.

One of the doctors that came by during that long day, a psychologist, warned him never to act the hero again. "I know you wanted to make a difference, but that's how the casualties increase. Best practice? Run in the other direction," said the old man. He reeked of cigarette smoke. Owen realized that because of how he was found, pistol-whipped and unconscious, everyone believed he'd attempted to intercede. The relief of this realization was brief and quickly replaced by the guilt of letting people think he was heroic when he was actually a coward.

A doctor was in the room with him talking about ordering an MRI. Owen looked out the window at the setting sun. He put his legs over the side of the bed and stood up. "OK, I'm going now," he said. "Where are my clothes?"

"Are you sure you're OK?" the doctor asked. "We'd like to run a few more tests."

"Yeah, I'm OK. You folks took good care of me."

"We were considering having you stay overnight."

"I won't be doing that," he said. "Where are my clothes?"

The mayor of Westwend, Rita Morse, had called the hospital and asked them to let her know when Owen would be released so she could send a car to take him home. The doctor went to call for Owen's ride, and he got dressed. There were a couple of aches and pains. The snack stand had cut his left side pretty badly. There were stitches and a dressing on it. Otherwise, he really could have gone straight to his house instead of going through a day of tests.

Standing out front of the hospital in the cool evening, he managed to bum a cigarette off a nervous-looking middle-aged woman who told him her husband had been in a car accident. She even lit the smoke for him with shaking hands before returning inside. The cigarette tasted of her grief. He threw it on the ground and took deep breaths of fresh air. Eventually, a police car from Westwend pulled up. The window came down and the officer waved to him. Owen knew the cop from him bringing his kids to the library.

The first thing he did upon arriving home was to find the bottle of bourbon in the kitchen cabinet and make himself a drink—ice and a little water—his usual. Then he sat at the table with his drink and wept for a good half hour. Eventually, he dried his eyes and forced himself to think of other things. He decided to go to work the next day, which was a decision not to have another bourbon. He had a sense he had to get back to himself, knowing the day's impact had been fierce enough to blow him off course for the rest of his life.

Until then, he'd never really considered the life he'd made in Westwend to be all it was cracked up to be, but after what he'd been through, he now thought of it as very sweet. He'd inherited his parents' house, free of charge. He was working in his hometown, in a job that utilized his college degrees. He had no lover or spouse to care for or about. No relatives in close proximity. The people who came to the library were pleasant enough, and some he liked immensely. He had time to read and to think in peace. He wondered if there would ever be anything important to him beside those things.

He finished his bourbon, and felt almost relaxed. An image of Helen smiling at him was trying to edge its way into his thoughts. He fought it and kept it at bay. "I'm exhausted," he said aloud. Getting to his feet, he leaned against the table before pushing off and heading for the bedroom. His clothes fell where they would. Almost asleep, he managed to slip into a pair of blue gym shorts and a yellow T-shirt.

The cool sheet, the marsh-like mattress, the familiar rough army blanket, caused him to sigh with comfort. He curled up on his side, a classic fetal position, and closed his eyes. As soon as he was in the dark, he sensed the stirring of dreams at the edges of his consciousness. The promise of oblivion came on and rid him of the tension of grief and fear. He was nearly out when the gash on his left side announced it was going to make a nuisance of itself. Eventually, the pain forced him onto his back just before sleep.

He came to. It was dark. He closed his eyes to see if he could return to his dreams and realized he was lying on his back, something he always made an effort not to do. He felt a sense of panic and tried to roll onto his right side. Although his command to himself was clear, and he seemed completely awake, he remained inert. He tried to wiggle his toes and couldn't. His breathing became erratic. A state of paralysis encased his entire body.

He cried out, not even thinking who might hear him, but his voice was stunted and filtered down to a bark-like whisper.

He hadn't experienced it since he was sixteen, but he knew what was happening. Immediately, he controlled his breathing—in for a four count, hold for eight, and then exhale. It was clear to him now, he was awake in a dream, not that it was enough to allow him to turn on his side, which he wanted more than anything in the world. It came back to him from twenty plus years earlier. His method of escape was to concentrate on his left pinky finger and try to get it to move ever so slightly. If he could just get that going, he could spread the movement through his body and break free from sleep. His pinky didn't respond. He switched to his big toe.

He wasted energy trying to move, exerting his will. His exhaustion finally stopped him from struggling within and he rested. Time passed, and then he felt something different happening. Not sure what it was, he wondered if he was dying. His body, though still paralyzed, was flooded with a strange sensation of lightness as he slowly slipped the clutches of gravity and floated toward the ceiling. Fear rose in him and he flailed his arms. Miraculously, they moved, and so did his legs. He was hovering in midair. Somehow, without even thinking to do it, he turned so he was looking down at his bed and his sleeping body. The scene was lit by a pale blue glow emanating from him.

At this point, he knew he should have been really frightened, but he felt not the least bit of worry. He noticed that his body, asleep in the bed below him, was breathing peacefully, and he gave himself over completely to the will of whatever was taking him up. The ceiling was no barrier in his ethereal state, and he rose through it, through the attic. He saw the moon shining in the attic window.

Then he found himself on the sidewalk in front of his house in his gym shorts and T-shirt—no shoes. The wind was as high as it had been the previous morning on his way to the library. It rustled the trees and sounded like running water. Owen's hair was tossed in the gale, and he knew he should have felt colder in such meager clothes. He looked down and could see through himself, just barely. Holding up his left hand, he saw the outline of the full moon through it. For all intents and purposes, he might as well have been a ghost.

And yet he could smell the spring night, heard the insects buzzing at the streetlight two houses down. Creepers sang and a night bird, far off, cried shrilly. A dog barked. He looked around and saw the living room light on in his next-door neighbor's house. Mrs. Hultz, seventy-five, who'd lived there his entire life, had recently confided in him that she never slept anymore. Instead, she drank gin and watched old mystery movies all night. Up the street, he saw the Blims' dog, Hecate, a mad Sheltie—in silhouette by moonlight—shitting on the Rogerses' lawn. Music came from some house, Nat King Cole, singing "Too Young." Owen took a few steps and felt as if he were gliding along the sidewalk. The movement was strange but pleasant for its unexpected lightness.

Since he took the entire experience to be a dream, he decided to draw closer to Mrs. Hultz's house and see what she was watching. The lighted window looked in over her shoulder. She sat in an old armchair upholstered with pink flowers. He saw her blue-white hair, the frame of her enormous glasses, and her arm bending, bringing the crystal gin to her lips. One glance at the TV, and he saw she was watching some old black-and-white movie. The quiet scene was a tableau of loneliness, but Owen felt it peaceful. There was a quick flash of Orson Welles's face emerging from the shadows, and he knew it was Carol Reed's *The Third Man*. Upon noticing Welles, he heard, very faintly, as if being played by a mosquito, the sound of zither music. He leaned his head closer to the window to better hear it. The classic tune came much clearer. In the next second, he realized he was leaning through the side of the house into Mrs. Hultz's living room like something from a cartoon. The experience made him shudder, which shook loose a memory of Helen dead behind the counter. In an instant, he was reeled in, rolled up, and everything went black.

3

THE NEXT MORNING, Owen ate breakfast and drank his coffee at the kitchen table instead of stopping for a roll. He'd plotted out on his phone a new route that didn't take him anywhere near the Busy Bee. There was one lone sparrow on the feeder. The weather was cool and breezy but the sun was bright. On any other morning, he'd have thought it a perfect day, but now he thought of nothing except for what had happened to him the night before. He'd obviously had an episode of lucid dreaming, but the look of the dream was sharper, as were his senses during it. It was a twin for real life, except he was some kind of spirit who could pass through the walls of houses and was truly conscious while doing it. He promised himself he would write down the experience as soon as he returned from work that evening. He put on the brown suit. As it grew time to leave, he felt an ice ball forming in his chest. He hoped not to speak to anybody about the death of Helen Roan.

At the first corner on the walk to town, he turned west onto another tree-lined street that looked like the one he lived on. There was something "skulking" about the fact he had changed his route. He felt like a thief in the night, and walked swiftly, keeping his eyes on the cracked concrete. There came a spot where he had to walk along a dirt road that led into the shadows beneath the cedars and blackjack oaks. It was as if all those things he didn't want to think about might be hiding in ambush behind the trees and underbrush. He heard their murmuring, the distant gunshot, and caught, in a side glance, Helen darting into a thicket. He finally came to the old railroad tracks and crossed them. A few steps later and he was clear of the woods, walking across the field of weeds toward the library.

Owen spent the morning on his office computer. First, he checked the local TV listings and found that *The Third Man* had actually been on the previous night. Then he read up on lucid dreaming and the astral plane. Everything he read had a tangential connection to what he'd experienced, but none of the experiences of others, in their descriptions, were close to his. He determined that what happened through the night was an out-of-body experience, an OBE. He'd read on more than one site that the phenomenon could be brought on by a head injury or great stress. He rubbed the wicked bruised bump on his jaw and envisioned a type of spirit persona leaving his body in order to wander the night world of reality, not dreams. The experience of a phantom—a silent, incorporeal witness to the workings of the world. As this conclusion dawned on him, he heard the chimes at the library's front door. It would be the first patron of the day.

He walked out to the front desk to see a man in a tweed jacket and dark glasses standing with a camera in his hands. Before Owen could speak, the man said, "I'd like to ask you about the robbery at the Busy Bee." He leaned his elbows on the counter, trying to appear familiar.

"I gave a statement to the police yesterday at the hospital," said Owen. "You can go to the station and check it out. Use that for your copy. I'm not offering any interviews."

"Not even for your local paper? People want to hear about you. You're a hero for trying to help."

"I'm not a hero," said Owen. "The whole thing happened so fast, I was hit in the face and unconscious before I even knew what was going on. I was a helpless bystander. Seriously. Go write that for the paper. It's the truth," he said, knowing full well it wasn't quite.

"I'll take it," said the reporter. "That's something no one else is writing." With this, he lifted the camera and snapped a quick shot of Owen.

"These are business hours," said the librarian in his sternest voice.

The man backed away toward the door. "Thanks," he said. The chimes sounded again and he was gone.

The remainder of the afternoon was dead, as if the library's usual patrons assumed the place was closed from having heard the news about the robbery. It was fine by Owen. He took up the usual work chores—reshelving, sending overdue notices, and weeding the collection for books that could be sacrificed to make room for newer books. This was the most difficult part of his job. He held in his hands a book from the children's section with duct tape holding it together. Even with all the obvious repairs, the cover was still half torn off from the spine. You could no longer see the illustration of an old woman in a rocking chair with kids gathered around her. The book was titled *The Daily Reader*. It was one of his favorites when he was a kid. It told stories about a family—husband and wife with a girl and a boy, six and seven, and a new baby. There was a story for every day of the year. Some were involved and some were very brief, like the entries in a person's diary. The reader got to be there for the big events and for the inconsequential. Owen, as a child, found the latter the nicest of all. Still, his warm memories of the story year he spent with that story family were not enough to stay his hand from tossing the decrepit volume into the trash bin. It was to be replaced on the shelf by a book about a boy who lived on an island and what happened when a coffin washed ashore. He hoped the kids who still came to the library would enjoy it as much as he'd enjoyed *The Daily Reader*.

A few minutes before closing, the chimes sounded again. Owen made his way out from amidst the stacks. There was nobody on the adult side of the library. He walked over to the children's section and saw a man standing with hands behind him, looking up at the mural on the back wall.

"Can I help you?" asked Owen. "We're about to close for the day."

The man turned and revealed himself to be Gerry Roan, owner of the Busy Bee and Helen's father. Owen was staggered. He couldn't even bring himself to say hello, although he'd known the man since they were both young. Instead, he shook his head as if vehemently denying something.

"I've come to see how you were. I heard you'd been put in the hospital," said Roan.

Owen found his voice. "Gerry, I'm so sorry about Helen."

"Are you OK?"

His spasm of denial ended and he was able to nod. "Don't worry about me. Is your wife holding up?"

"No, neither of us is very good. We can't sleep."

"I wish I'd been able to do something," said Owen.

"What can you do?" said Roan. "Life really doesn't make any sense. We all secretly know that. This guy was a drug maniac or something."

"Still . . ."

"I'm just glad you were there with her when it happened. She always admired you from the time she was young. I think it was because you had so many books," he said, and laughed.

Owen didn't react to the joke. An uncomfortable silence followed, and eventually Gerry Roan walked over to the librarian and hugged him. Without speaking, he left. The sound of his car starting and receding was followed by the peculiar tomb-like silence that settled down around the books at evening. The sunlight through the window then could be its most golden on the field for a brief few minutes. The thought of Roan's statement that Helen admired him because he had so many books came back to him, and he moved quickly to try to dispel his sorrow. The unfamiliar walk home through the woods spooked him. By the time he came out the other side, along the dirt road, night had fallen.

After dinner, he played the classical station on the radio. It turned out to be a big night for the music of Satie. Owen finished the bourbon and gave vent to all manner of bad notions, gave in to every paranoia, ran through the scene in the Busy Bee a dozen times behind his eyes. When it got late and he kept nodding off, his head banging once or twice against the kitchen table, even as drunk as he was, he knew it was time to surrender. He stumbled into the bedroom, knowing he'd have a rough time of it in the morning. Again, he forgot about the wound in his side, felt a jab as he was getting into bed, and had to switch to the right. He fell asleep almost instantly, but before he did, he managed to push himself onto his back, hoping to regain transit to the night world. His sleep was as dark as death, though. Not a shred of dream nor the fearful paralysis.

He woke but a few minutes later to the sound of the alarm clock. The nausea and headache were nothing compared to the fact that, as he was dressing for work, he remembered that today was going to be a ceremony for Helen. The body was still in the custody of the police for autopsy and would be for a few more days. Helen's parents didn't want to wait for the inevitable closure. Her father had mentioned it before leaving the library. "Awfully quick," Owen had thought, and put it out of his mind. The sudden, returning thought of it froze him where he sat on the edge of his bed, holding a pair of socks. He knew there was no way he could make it through the memorial and the looks and words, no matter how kind the citizens of Westwend. Owen was revealing himself to be more of a coward than even he'd suspected. Still, he dressed in his blue-gray suit and went to work, taking the new, secret route. He prayed no one would see him, and no one did.

His suffering induced by the bourbon subsided around midday. There were patrons at a steady pace, and a pile of kids came in after school to work on projects together. Some of the adults mentioned the robbery to him. The older folks knew better than to blurt it out in conversation but smiled wistfully and patted him on the shoulder as he checked out their books. For the first time in a long time, he left early. It's not like there was anyone around to evict, but he killed the lights and locked the door twenty minutes before closing.

After making it home without being spotted, Owen grabbed the rolled-up newspaper from where it was shoved into the iron scroll work of the porch banister. He staggered inside and shut and locked the door behind him. He dressed in his shorts and T-shirt. Curling up in a corner of the living room couch, he propped himself with his elbow against the pillowed arm, and turned on the light above his head. The front page of the *Westwend Tattler* had a large photo of the ceremony for Helen Roan from earlier in the day. Owen skipped it. On page two was his "confession" that he was no hero.

He felt so wronged by that one word—*confession*—as if he'd been leading the community on, been boasting about how he'd tried to disarm the murderer. He'd never claimed such a thing. All he was really guilty about was not telling everyone he was a straight-up coward, and who would go out of their way to say such a thing? The paper fell from his hands onto the floor. He rolled onto his back and stretched his legs out. His fingers just reached the light switch. In minutes he was mercifully out and lightly snoring.

4

THIS TIME THERE WAS no paralytic prelude; he began to ascend the instant he awoke in his sleep. Up through the attic like last time. Out through the roof on the left side, next to the chimney. And then he swept down as graceful as an angel and touched his feet lightly on the sidewalk. He wasn't overwhelmed by the sheer strangeness of the experience this time. The first thing he noticed was that it must be much later than when he'd lain upon the couch. The houses were all dark, save for Mrs. Hultz's. The moon was half of what it had been last he was on the night street. The sky was wondrously clear, with millions of stars.

He slipped weightlessly along the sidewalk, and this time when he got to the corner, he turned away from town and instead toward the park and the pine barrens. Why he was heading in that direction, he had no idea. When he passed the Blims' house, Hecate was lying on the front lawn, watching the street. Owen was afraid he'd be seen. He noticed that the dog did lift its head and sniff the air, but for once it didn't bark. A few houses along the way, he spotted a lit window and wondered what was going on behind it at that late hour. He changed course and swerved across the lawn to have a look.

The house was a ranch style with the windows close to the ground. Owen swore he wouldn't invade other people's homes in his invisible state. As far as spying on them, though, for some reason, that was another matter. He was infinitely curious about how people lived. In the well-lit room was a boy in red pajamas, somewhere between the ages of eight and ten. He was sitting at a small round table with two chairs. In between those two seats lay a chessboard. Owen watched as the boy made a move, ushering his queen from behind the defense of horses to attack. Then the boy got up, went to the seat opposite, sat and stared at the board, and made a move for that side. He was his own opponent. *Familiar,* thought the librarian. He'd never seen the boy before, and made a note in his memory to check if he was a patron of the library. He thought it might be worthwhile to get in some newer chess books.

He traveled on, toward the end of the road, and just before the entrance to the park, he passed a driveway with a running car parked in it. He peered into the vehicle and saw, by the light of an e-reader in her hand, a young woman. She was fast asleep behind the wheel. In the dark back seat, there was a fat-faced baby, smiling and kicking its legs. Owen surmised it was some failed attempt to get the child to sleep.

These acts he was witnessing would be seen by no one else. Night, its solitude and cover, gave a thrilling aspect to the mundane—like knowing a secret. What the secret was, he had no idea. But as he came to the end of the sidewalk at the entrance to the park, and took a step onto the gravel path, he formed a theory that people were probably most themselves after sunset. He walked along the path through the park, just east of the baseball diamond. It came to him that he didn't want to wind up in the pine barrens in his phantom state. But a few feet on, he saw a waist-high sign that was a wooden arrow. It pointed the way to the cemetery of St. Ifritia.

That's how he found out why he was there. He'd come to pay his respects. He was in the cemetery where the event for Helen Roan had been held. A funeral without a body. He took the path to search for the grave marker awaiting her remains. His pale blue glow lit the headstones just enough so he could read them. As he crept along, he realized he was fulfilling some inner directive to atone for missing Helen's memorial. He also became conscious of the fact that he was walking at night in a cemetery as a kind of ghost.

He came to a gravesite near a tree bedecked with pink and white ribbons, and hung with strings tied to now-deflated balloons. The waist-high marble marker in front of the tree read IN MEMORY OF HELEN ROAN and gave her dates. At the foot of the marker was a gaping hole awaiting its cargo.

With head bowed, he stood in silence and made his peace with Helen Roan. "I wish I could have saved you," he whispered. He expected her spirit to fly out of the tree and admonish him for being a selfish coward. He occasionally had to remind himself that it wasn't a fantasy land he now traveled but reality. That was the strangest part. He stood there for a time, hands folded in front of him, until he got the impression someone was watching him. Turning quickly, he saw no one. Slowly and quietly, he moved away from Helen's headstone and back toward the path that led to the park.

Moving clear of the rows of headstones, he turned and saw a figure, glowing pale blue like himself, moving toward him from a distance of five or six rows. Owen ran, but he found that running in the night world was like running on the moon. Because his spirit form was lighter, each thrust of the leg shot you way up but not necessarily very far forward. Owen leaped house high but was slowed in his escape. The other glowing figure caught up and told him to stop. When he floated slowly down from on high, the figure made to take his hand to ground him, but the hand passed right through his.

She laughed as he made contact with the ground and bounced up a foot and a half.

"Who are you?" asked Owen, finally settling and turning to see her. He could tell it was a woman through the pale blue glow. She wore a robe and a nightgown like Sleeping Beauty in the mural but with a much shorter hem and a lace collar instead of décolletage. Her hair was short, and he couldn't tell because of its incandescence what color it would be in the waking world.

"I'm a sleeper like you," she said. And in that instant, he was called back, seemingly yanked by the collar, all the way across the park and back up his street, into his bed.

At breakfast the next morning, instead of his usual contemplation of the rescue of Sleeping Beauty, he tried to recall the face of the woman he met in the night world. Another person having an out-of-body experience? He'd never considered the possibility. She called herself a "sleeper." He wondered how many sleepers there were in the area, and if she might have recognized him from the library. On one hand, he found it wondrous that sleeping people could shed their corporeal selves and rise up to meet as spirits or phantoms in the real world. On the other hand, the thought carried a tinge of disappointment in that he'd treasured the quiet solitude of the night world.

He took off for work along his secret route, impatient

to be at the end of the day and to experience the phenomenon again. It was his plan next time to more carefully observe and to write down what he experienced. Nothing much happened at the library. Mrs. Hultz arrived at noon to read to whatever toddlers were brought in by their mothers or fathers for story time. No takers showed, so she waylaid Owen with her tales of distant relations and medical issues. Just before she had mercy and left his office, though, she told him she'd seen in that day's newspaper an article about the gunman from the Busy Bee. The authorities didn't have a name for him yet, but they mentioned a small black tattoo of a cross in a circle on his wrist that they believed to be a gang affiliation sign.

"I saw it," said Owen.

"Gangs in Westwend," said Mrs. Hultz, and shook her head.

5

OWEN STRUGGLED AGAINST THE inertia of his body for what felt like an hour before being released to the night. Out on the street, he decided to head toward town, hoping since there were more people in that direction, there would be more sleepers. He desperately wanted answers about the dark world he roamed. A few steps along the sidewalk and he noticed something up ahead. A pale blue glow, passing through the wall of a neighbor's house.

The man who owned the house was a forbidding fellow who never waved when Owen greeted him, yelled at the kids not to play on the sidewalk in front of his place, and had a nasty-looking pit bull. Although Owen had promised himself he wouldn't spy on people in their homes beyond looking in the lighted windows, his curiosity got the better of him. *What's the point of this special power if not to see what is otherwise unseen?*

He trod across the man's lawn and went to the side of the house where he'd seen the other glowing figure enter through the wall next to the chimney. *I'm not only a coward but now a pervert as well,* he thought as he took a step forward and passed through the wall into a darkened dining room. The first thing he noticed was the light in the next room. He crept, though he didn't have to, to the doorway and peered in. There was the man, a grimace upon his face and his hands covering his eyes.

Owen toured the downstairs—the kitchen, the bathroom, a disheveled bedroom. The place was poorly taken care of. There were dishes in the sink, and dust balls as silent as Owen rolled along the wooden floor of the hallway. He wondered why he'd decided to invade the man's house. What he found was a life as lonely as his own, though not as neat, which he wasn't sure counted for anything. Instead of wonder, he'd discovered a shabby reality.

There was one more room at the end of the hall. A light from inside streamed out into the dark through the sliver of door that was ajar. Inside the room he could faintly hear the sound of rhythmic, raspy breaths, or perhaps some mechanical device laboring steadily away. He was intrigued enough to pass through the door. In front of him was a bed holding an emaciated woman. She was dressed in red satin pajamas and had a green kerchief around her head. She slept peacefully, breathing in and out with the help of a machine standing next to the bed. There was a plastic mask covering her mouth and nose with a tube attaching it to the device. A small table in the corner of the room was crowded with pill bottles and a vase containing a red rose. Although Owen really couldn't see what she looked like, he saw enough of her cheeks and forehead to see her color was ashen.

At her feet lay the "menacing" pit bull with his head resting tenderly upon her ankles, breathing in time with the breathing machine. Owen felt his emotions well up—first, surprise at the unexpected nature of what he discovered behind the walls of the house; second, his heart went out to the dog and the man and the poor woman. He knew now why the fellow didn't want kids hanging out making a racket on the sidewalk, and why he was always too preoccupied to wave back or say hello.

Owen heard the heavy steps of the home owner in the hallway behind him. He felt a burst of panic in his chest, forgetting his invisibility. Turning quickly, he looked for a place to hide. A pale blue arm aglow like Owen's appeared from out of the center of the closet door in the corner and motioned for him to follow. Just as his neighbor entered the room, he stepped through the closet door. In the dark, he saw the other sleeper pass through the wall of the house and out into the night. He followed.

At the back of the property two houses down, just in front of a line of tall hedges, the dimly glowing sleeper sat at an old picnic table. Owen drew cautiously closer until he could make out it was the woman he'd met at the cemetery the previous night.

"We meet again," he whispered.

"You don't have to whisper," she said in a normal tone. "Most in the waking world can't hear you."

"May I sit down?" he asked.

She motioned with a sweep of her arm for him to do so. Now that he was just the table's width away and neither of them was moving, he got a better look at her face. It was still difficult to read detail, what with the glow, but he could tell she must be a little older than he was, perhaps seven or eight years, in her mid-forties. She was a big woman, not heavy but solid, with broad shoulders. As he scooted into the seat opposite her, he noted she was an inch or so taller than him. Her face was deadpan, and her hair, which he had believed to be short, actually came to her shoulders and in front was cut into bangs. It now revealed its waking-world color as dark brown or black.

"How did you get here?" she asked, and the earlier deadpan expression turned into a smile.

"I seriously think it was from a knock on the head," he told her.

"I've heard of it before. OBEs are uncommon, in and of themselves, but that scenario among those who travel by night is not. Trauma, physical or mental, can set off an episode."

"My name is Owen," he said, and put his hand out across the table.

She put hers out as well and the two open palms passed through each other.

"That didn't go so well," he said.

"Sleepers can't touch." She drew back her arm and said, "I'm Melody."

"How did you get here?"

"I can get here anytime I want, through mental training and meditation. I studied with some very knowledgeable people. In most cases, I can also control when I return to my body. I bet you can't."

"True," said Owen. "I could get pulled back to myself like a yo-yo at any second."

"Because you're an accidental sleeper."

"Accidental?"

She nodded. "Your ability to achieve an OBE could disappear at any time and you might never achieve it again."

"Well, it's kind of strange. I might not mind."

"It's like being a ghost, isn't it?" she said.

"Is that what you like about it?"

"That, and the quiet nature of the night, seeing into things you're blocked from while awake. I've always been a loner at heart."

"Me too," he said. "Why were you in that house?"

"I used to work with the woman and wondered how she was getting on."

"Apparently not so well," said Owen. "Are you from this neighborhood?"

"Not too far. Down in town, more near the stores."

"Why did you follow me in the cemetery the other night?"

"I had a feeling you were new by the way you were trying to run." She laughed. "I wanted to tell you there are some things you need to know about being a sleeper if you want to stay safe. I was trying to warn you. Someone did it for me, so you need to pass it on when you encounter a novice."

"I'd appreciate your help."

"OK, then follow me." She stood, and leaped in one smooth bound over the hedge behind her.

In her nightgown and robe, she looked like an angel, ascending and falling. For some reason, it made him smile. He slid off the bench and followed her with a bound. He landed in someone else's backyard. Melody was already moving toward the side of the house. Afraid to run to catch up, he walked quickly, and saw her pass through a gate leading to the front and the street. She waited under a streetlight, and as he caught up, she said, "You know, since you could be called back any time, if that happens, I'll meet you at the picnic table we just left."

"Agreed," said Owen.

"Like I said, being you're here due to a bump on the

head, you may find that one night you're no longer able to achieve this state. The whole thing works mysteriously. Scientists take MRIs of people experiencing an OBE, and register what the brain does, but they really don't understand what's going on. Of course, they don't heed the spiritual nature of it, and that's definitely a big part of it—at least from my experience." She turned and walked, with him beside her.

"How did you acquire the ability to achieve an OBE at will?"

"We'll get to that, but I want to fill you in about the dangers now, while we have the chance. With your limited experience, you probably think the sum total is running around the night streets of the waking world and playing invisible hide-and-seek."

"There's more to it?"

"A lot more," she said, and stopped. He could tell she was listening intently by her stillness and the position of her head. "This way," she eventually said. At the corner, they turned again toward the park and cemetery. "There are creatures and entities inhabiting this phase of being, the night world, you need to steer clear of."

"Entities?"

"Even though it feels like we are walking the streets of the waking world, which we are, in this dimension, or astral plane, or whatever you want to call the reality that accommodates us, there are other players."

"For instance?"

"Well, have you ever heard of the silver cord?"

"I ran into a discussion of OBEs and such on the internet after I made my first journey the other night. Sort of a silver bungee that tethers you to your body. Right?"

"More or less," said Melody. "If there were illustrations with the information, there probably were depictions of the cord emanating from the sleeping body's forehead and connecting at the spiritual form's forehead. At times, you'll see it as emanating from the chest or the back. The odd thing is, I don't have one and neither do you and neither do most I've met. And yet all of my teachers—great adepts—swear everyone has one whether it can be seen or not."

He nodded as they crossed the street to the park entrance.

"OK, there are a number of ways the cord might be severed while the spirit is about in the night. If that happens, the sleeper's body will die. But the spirit body adrift in the night world atrophies, shrivels, and becomes an evil entity with only one purpose: to sever the cords of other travelers."

"The misery-loves-company school of retribution?"

"Yes. But it's not like a conscious will on their part. It's more like they become an aspect of—if you can comprehend this—the spiritual ecosystem of the world we move through."

"How do you distinguish them from regular sleepers?

"They glow like us. They look like us in every aspect except their eyes are cold. You've got to be fairly close to them to see this, though. If someone approaches and they have an empty affect, jump away quickly. They're earthbound and have lost the power to leap like we can."

"What happens if you don't notice their eyes?"

"Their fingers are capable of piercing your incorporeal form, usually through the chest, and unhooking your cord. And an instant later, you're one of them. Sometimes they hunt in packs. Remember, there's nothing human about them. Whatever seems human, speech, facial expression, gait, is all unconscious mimicry."

"I thought sleepers couldn't touch. So, how do they unhook your silver cord? It doesn't make sense."

"I can't explain it," she said. "The night world has somehow allowed this to happen. My teacher told me to think of it as a mutation promoting evolutionary change in that it sets up a serious challenge to the quality of sleepers. I'm not sure what she meant."

"Have you ever seen someone lose their cord?"

"No. But what I've heard from those who've witnessed it, it's accompanied by a stifled gasp, like an expression of great agony, inhibited by the fact that the sleeper becomes something wholly other."

"Jesus," said Owen. "The entire thing is like a convoluted nightmare. How often do you run into cord-cutters?"

"I travel every night, so maybe every couple of months. Because I've been crossing over to the world of night since I was a teenager, I can hear them as whispering static at a bit of a distance. You, though, will have no warning."

"It's a lot scarier now than it was."

"Look up," she said. They were in the park and heading toward the cemetery. He looked up, but instead of following her pointing hand, he looked into her eyes. She smiled. "Don't worry, I'm not a cutter."

"I wasn't looking at you for that reason," he said.

"Then why?"

"The glow makes it difficult for me to clearly see your face."

"There's nothing important to see," said Melody. "But out there, across the field, do you see the yellow cloud hovering a few feet above the ground?"

He shifted his gaze and saw what looked like a small cloud come down to earth, wisps of a sulfurous shade roiling and drifting slowly above the field. "What is it?"

"The miasma. If any part of it touches you, you'll be disintegrated—erased out of existence. Not just in the night world but in your waking life, and the strangest thing is that no one will remember you. It'll be as if you never existed in the waking world. All I know is that this cuts deeply across many dimensions and through many planes of existence, but reality will somehow rearrange itself and blot out the wound you are, and no one—even your parents—will be the wiser. The only memory of you that will still exist will be with other sleepers who knew you in the night world."

"Sounds like a fairy tale," said Owen.

"Don't worry about it making sense," she said. "You've got to keep an eye out for the miasma. It's slow-moving but stealthy and is attracted to sleepers. The good news is it can easily be outmaneuvered. The bad is you can't hear it approaching. I once saw a sleeper taken down by it. It looked horribly painful and slow as the ethereal body went up in smoke. It looks insubstantial but once it's got you, that's it. So, keep your wits and watch your back."

Owen felt his hair stand up and a chill run down his spine. He turned quickly, only to wake in bed with the first light of dawn showing through the bedroom blinds.

6

DESPITE ALL THE GALLIVANTING around through the night, Owen felt unusually refreshed, as if his sleep had been deeper and more sustained than normal. He was often still yawning and stretching until he had a cup of black coffee, but on this day, he jumped out of bed, feeling a reserve of energy. While sitting at the kitchen table, having breakfast, staring out at the birds and the feeder that needed restocking, his mind was on Melody and the night world. The prospect of visiting it again excited and scared him.

Melody presented herself as some kind of adept, like a guru of OBEs. He considered the possibility that she was—even though he'd run into her on successive nights—just a dream, along with the rest of his sleeping adventures. But he had to admit everything about the experiences seemed utterly real. He felt that he needed to check something he'd witnessed only in the night world against the reality of the waking world. The first thing he thought of was that he'd been to Helen Roan's grave as a sleeper but not when awake. He would go to the cemetery after work and see if there was a tree with ribbons and deflated balloons near her grave. If it turned out to be so, then he would have some kind of verification that the night world was legitimate. It was Saturday and the library closed early at three o'clock, so he'd have time to walk over before dark.

On his way to work that morning, he went through all Melody had told him about the night world. He had a fleeting thought as to whether he should trust her. Who was to say that she was not some evil entity drawing him into a situation from which he'd never return? He weighed what he knew. It was the reason he was trying to see the details of her face. He trusted his ability to read whether people were good or not. From what he'd seen, he had no reason to doubt her. As he was walking along, lost in his thoughts, he came up short at the very last second before running into someone.

The neighbor whose house he was in the previous night, the man with the ailing wife, stood before him. The fellow was dragging his garbage can to the curb. In an unguarded moment, Owen blurted out, "Hello. How's your wife doing?" and instantly regretted opening his mouth. The man's stony expression melted, his glaring eyes went soft, and he said, "As good as can be expected." Surprised he'd gotten a response, Owen moved quickly around him and down the sidewalk before he could make another blunder. He turned and said to his neighbor, "Have a good day," and the fellow lifted a hand to wave and smiled. Only then did Owen realize he was trembling. A few more feet farther down the sidewalk, and he wondered if this was the proof he was contemplating at breakfast. Something verified from the night world to the waking world.

By the time he reached the library, he realized his encounter was really not proof of anything except that the man had a wife. The question he'd asked and the answer the man gave could mean a million different things. It didn't necessarily indicate that his neighbor's wife was relegated to bed, every breath perhaps her last. Maybe she simply had a cold or her mother had passed away or their dog had died. Owen would still have to make his way to the cemetery that afternoon to check the tree near Helen's grave. For the time being, he put the thought out of his head.

It turned out to be a beautiful spring day, and at lunchtime he went outside and sat on the bench. There were no patrons inside, and he'd finished his important work. The calm stillness of the afternoon was suddenly broken by a sound like an asthmatic demon. "What the hell is it?" he thought, and turned to look up the road in the direction of the din. He saw Mrs. Hultz's dilapidated 1990 maroon Cadillac Brougham. The car was in about the same shape as its owner. He was beginning to wonder if Mrs. Hultz's longevity, seventy-five years, had something to do with the gin.

She pulled up in front of the building and her front right tire went up on the sidewalk. Parking the car like that, she turned it off, then opened the door, hinges crying out. Owen waved and she approached him, waddling along in a blueberry-colored skirt and jacket, white corsage pinned to the lapel. Her shoes were flats and her hat was a pillbox type he'd not seen worn since he was young and his parents would take him to church. Mrs. Hultz was radically bowlegged. Without saying hello to him, she walked up and took a seat on the bench.

"I see you're goofing off on the job," she said.

"Just too nice out today. What are you up to?"

"I came to see you."

"To what do I owe the honor?"

"I've got a secret to share."

"Well?"

"I was at the gas station, and the attendant was filling my tank—a young guy—big and burly with a long beard and a rat's nest of long hair. Anyway, when he brings me back my credit card and the receipt to sign, the cuff of his shirt rides up a little and I see he has a small black tattoo of a circle with a cross in it on his wrist."

"So, you're thinking he's part of the gang you told me

about the other day?"

"What else?"

"And?

"We need to know what these people are up to."

"Why?"

"Because they're dangerous. The one who shot the poor Roan girl was obviously on drugs of some kind."

"Did the police report that?" asked Owen.

"Not yet, but come on. It was the dumbest robbery ever. Zero planning. The guy was desperate for money to get high."

"You should have your own TV show."

"I'm not joking. As an upstanding member of the community, you need to help me."

"Help you what?"

She stood up and started walking back to her car. Without turning she said, "I'll be here at three to pick you up."

"Why?"

"A stakeout."

He tried to protest but she acted as if she couldn't hear him. The door squealed open again, she got in, started the invalid vehicle that wheezed, and lurched away.

At three, good to her word, Mrs. Hultz was there at the curb, waiting for him, when he locked the front door of the building. Owen resigned himself to his fate. When he got in the passenger side, she handed him a peanut butter and jelly sandwich.

"What's this for?" he said.

"I thought you might be hungry after work."

He really wanted to be on his way, cutting through the woods and across the old tracks, so he could get to the cemetery before dark, but at the same time he remembered what great friends Mrs. Hultz had been with his mother. He thought of all the times he played with her daughters, Ellie, Sue, and Lila, when they were young. She was there for his mom through her decline and final illness, even more so than Owen and his dad were. For that, he kept quiet and ate peanut butter and jelly.

"It's going to be hard to be stealthy with this car," he said to her.

"Are you kidding?" she said. "It runs like a charm."

"Which do you think is in better shape? You or the Caddy?"

"What kind of question is that, Owen? Are you being disrespectful?" she asked, and laughed.

In three minutes, they were in the center of Westwend, a block of storefronts on either side of Cobb Street—a traffic light, a bar, two churches. She pulled into the grocery store parking lot, which was across from the gas station they were supposedly staking out. She kept the car running but put it in Park.

"Do you see the guy?" he asked. There were a couple of young men pumping gas for customers.

She shook her head. "It's not one of them. I wonder if he's already gone for the day. That would be a shame."

"I can wait for a little while," he said, "but I have to get back before it gets too late. I have an appointment at four."

"Girlfriend?" she asked. "Who is it?"

"No, not a girlfriend."

"A boyfriend?" she asked.

"No, I'm currently not engaged in a relationship of any kind."

"Why not?"

"Too much bother."

"You might as well join a monastery," she said.

"There's more to life than relationships."

"No, there isn't. You've got to get out there and meet someone."

He was about to tell her off when she grabbed his arm and said, "Look, the guy coming out the bay door of the garage. That's him."

He saw a large man, 6′2″ at least, as she'd described earlier, with long tangled hair and a bushy beard. They watched as he made his way along the sidewalk and then turned off Cobb onto Margrave Street. Mrs. Hultz put the car in Reverse and backed out of the parking spot. When she shifted into Drive, the car made a sound like the transmission had fallen out. They were off at a blistering ten miles an hour.

"He'll be in the next state by the time you catch up to him," said Owen.

When they made the turn onto Margrave, the tires squealed.

"Do you see him?" she asked, and slowed to prowl along the suburban street.

As she spoke, the car passed by a house with more land than the usual half an acre, set back among pine trees. The path to the front door was visible from the car. The gas station attendant stood on the porch and stared out at them as they crept by. Owen saw him at the last second and tried to cover his face with his hand.

"He's seen us. Hit the gas," he said.

She jammed her foot on the gas and the car released a blast and a cloud of black smoke before crawling away.

"Are you worried about him having noticed your car?" asked Owen.

Mrs. Hultz shrugged. "I've got the old gat at home."

"The old gat?"

"My husband's gun."

"Oh, Christ," he said. "Do you know how to use it?"

"How hard could it be?"

"You're a dangerous woman," he said, and then asked if she'd drop him off at the cemetery on the way home.

"Socializing?" she asked.

7

MRS. HULTZ DROPPED HIM off at the entrance to the park. He walked past the baseball diamond and along the gravel path leading to the cemetery. Taking a hard look at the scenery, he compared it to how it had looked late at night. When he reached the acreage of burials, he traveled aimlessly up and down the rows with the sun slowly falling. His mind wandered, thinking about Mrs. Hultz with a gun. After a little more than an hour had passed—out of the corner of his eye—as he lurched along an aisle of headstones, he saw the name HELEN ROAN.

The setting looked different by the light of the waking world. The grave was no longer empty and already there was grass sprouting on the packed mound of the burial. There was a tree behind the headstone when he'd visited it by night, but there was no sign of ribbons or deflated balloons hanging from its branches. Upon seeing this, he had no choice but to conclude that his so-called OBEs were merely a recurring dream. "Who would have a ceremony for a dead daughter at an open grave in front of a tree with pink ribbons and balloons?" Owen said aloud, admonishing his own foolishness. With that thought, his perception of being a sleeper went from freedom to suffocation. A sinking deeper into oblivion.

As he walked down the last row of graves on the way to the gravel path, he saw, pressed by the wind against the chain link fence separating the cemetery from the park, a finger's length of frayed pink ribbon. He strode off course to where it was trapped and took it. Rubbing it between his fingers, he sought to verify its reality. In his imagination he saw the cemetery workers filling in the grave and cutting down the decorations. He wondered if there could have been enough time for all that since the memorial for Helen. It had been windy lately, and a shred might have easily blown free. He was so pleased to have found it. The little piece of material evidence confirmed his faith in Melody and what she'd been telling him.

Across the picnic table that night, he told her about the death of Helen Roan, the hit in the head that made him a sleeper, and his test, comparing the girl's night grave and beribboned tree to the same scene in daylight. The two of them glowed pale blue against the dark, talking in low voices, not because they had to but because that's the way they would have spoken on a spring night in the waking world. Then he showed Melody the piece of pink ribbon he'd found against the fence and spoke about how it immediately mended his perception of her and of being a sleeper.

"Owen, you have to understand," she said. "At night, when we rise up from our sleeping bodies and walk the neighborhood, the world isn't exactly like waking life. There are things that can influence the night world. You already know it has its own predators, the cutters and the miasma. Sometimes, something from your dreams can slip into the night world. 99.9 percent of what you're seeing and experiencing is the same as the waking world, but there is a small percentage of times where you'll run into something inexplicable. Something concocted by your ego or id or whatever those processes are that take place in the shadiest corners of your imagination. Nothing to worry about until it happens," said Melody.

"The very fact it's possible, though," said Owen, "makes it difficult to believe *any* aspect of the night world."

"Everything is mutable, not exactly what it's made out to be, and neither completely one way or the other. There's always room for change and speculation, even in the waking world. It's part of the human condition. The same goes for the night."

He nodded and paused before asking, "What are we going to do tonight?"

"Let's visit some of your fellow citizens."

"You mean go into people's houses? Isn't that wrong?"

"You were in your neighbor's house the other night. I didn't see you hesitate." Melody pointed two houses up the street.

"I was chasing you," he said.

"Did you learn anything?"

"I suppose, but spying on people isn't my thing."

"Don't think of it as spying. It's a unique opportunity to see the intimate aspects of others' lives."

"Shouldn't they be private?"

"For the most part, yes. As a sleeper, you have a special responsibility to see how people live, and to know their joy and suffering. There's nothing prurient about it. As a sleeper, you are called on to bear witness to the night."

"Then why would the police arrest someone for peeping in another's window?"

"That's in the waking world. You have other responsibilities there."

"Are you serious, Melody?" he asked. "That we're expected to bear witness? But are we supposed to do something about whatever suffering or evil or joy we encounter?"

"Sometimes, if we can. It's up to you."

"Vague."

"Come then," she said, and stood. She led him, again, over the hedge, through the adjoining backyard, and to the street. "Choose a house at random," she told him.

"Do people have to be awake? Does there need to be a lit window?"

She shook her head. "Any house is fine. Discoveries abound."

Ten minutes later, they stood in a darkened room, leaning over a crib, watching a baby sleep. Owen made as if to push the mobile above the child, a herd of zebras, into motion, but his hand passed through it.

"So sweet," said Melody.

They moved down the hall and found the parents' room. A young couple slept in one another's arms. The spring breeze blew in through the screen of the open window. A black dog in the corner of the room awoke and tracked the movements of the intruders. "Can it see us?" he asked.

"Maybe. Some can but not many." That said, the dog started barking—loud, low—and fierce.

"Someone's here," said the woman in the bed.

Her partner stirred and said, "What was that?"

Melody walked through the wall to the outside and Owen quickly followed. They stepped off from the second story and floated like feathers to the ground.

"What did you make of that one?" she asked.

"Peaceful until we showed up," he said.

A little while later, they spent some time in the attic

apartment of a young woman writing a book. She had sheets of butcher paper taped on the walls of the cramped room. Using a Flair pen, she wrote her lines around herself and became like a fly in a spider's web.

"Her name is Shiela Tobac," said Melody, as the woman sat at a small desk only two feet away from them, bobbing her head as she wrote longhand in a journal dedicated to notes about her massive story. She wore a green T-shirt and a green cardigan sweater, shorts, sneakers with thick yellow soles, and white basketball socks. Her movements around the room bordered on the athletic. Even when she stood reading from some section of the wall, she bounced on her toes, her long red hair swaying wildly.

"She looks like a hard worker," said Owen. "I mean she's up and she's down and traveling from one part of the room and its chapter to another corner to, I guess, check the continuity?"

"She's crossed the line between genius and insanity," said Melody.

"Heading in which direction?"

"Well, I come here now and then and try to find my way back into her story."

"What's it about?" he asked as the busy Shiela Tobac passed through them on the way to a distant chapter.

"Too much to get into," she said. "I wouldn't know

how to start telling you about it."

"I think she's amazing, living inside her creation," said Owen. By then, they were out on the rooftop. They stood at the edge and Owen waited for Melody to choose a way to go. Eventually, she leaped across the side yard and driveway below and landed on the roof next door. From there, she leaped again, high and at the peak of ascent almost weightless, jump after jump, all the way down the street. Ten houses in a row. He followed her, with a few stumbles. The last of those mishaps saw him trip and fall headfirst through the roof, through the second floor, to the living room of an abandoned house.

He landed in the middle of a candlelit scene. One man was sitting in a chair in a corner that the light could almost but not quite reach, his face and much of his body obscured. Two young men, just visible in the glow, were sitting in chairs facing the first man in the shadows. They gave him a satchel of money and he produced a plastic bag of large, live cicadas. The two traders immediately dug into their plastic bags, pulled out squirming specimens, and shoved them into their mouths. As they chewed, laughter spilled out of the darkness, and Owen leaped all the way to the roof.

When he caught up with Melody, she was sitting on a dormer a few houses down across the street, facing out into the pine barrens. No moon that night but a wealth of stars again. "Where did you go?" she said. "I thought you'd been called back." He told her about falling through the roof, and about the weird transaction of money for insects.

"I've seen it a few times lately," she said. "Some kind of new drug. Big with the wealthy. Massospora, it's called—a parasite that infects the rear ends of cicadas. It actually eats away their hind part and forms a shell around that area and produces a fungus. When ingested by humans, the fungus has the effects of psilocybin—like magic mushrooms. There's a component of the chemical makeup that's also an amphetamine."

"How do you know all this?"

"I spend all night looking over people's shoulders and reading what they read on the computer or in a book, I overhear conversations in dark corners, and I've seen quite a few of those drug sales going down in the last year or so."

"There's something wrong with it," said Owen.

"You think?" she said, and then they sat in silence for a while and took in the beautiful night. He asked her, "What's your life like during the day?"

"Oh, I work at a job. I have kids. I'm married. This year will be our fifteenth year."

"What's your husband's name?"

"Marcus."

"Does he know you're a sleeper?"

"Why should he? This is my private thing. Like Shiela Tobac's web of words."

"Have you moved through genius to insanity?" he asked.

"Only at the holidays when the in-laws show up."

They visited a veteran who couldn't sleep. A photo of him and his unit somewhere in the Middle East hung on the wall across the room from where he sat at a table. He smoked cigarettes one after the other, and had three packs stacked up on the table next to a neat pile of issues of *The Magazine of Fantasy and Science Fiction*. The copy in his hands was from 1999. The pages turned rhythmically and he silently moved his lips with each word. It wasn't so much as if he was taking in the story but more that the act of reading was a ritual that sustained him or took his mind off something.

From there, they went next door to where two old men had fallen asleep in front of the television—one in the recliner and one on the couch. Both sawed wood through late-night talk shows while the glow of the TV blended with the glow of Melody and Owen. On the hutch in the next room, barely visible in the dark, were photos that appeared to be from the old couple's wedding. The two burly men, much younger, wrapped in each other's arms, kissing, on the steps of a church, while friends and family threw rice. Their apartment was neat as a pin and there were shelves everywhere with classical music CDs and stereo records. In the corner of a room down the hall were an upright bass, an electric piano, and an array of five different saxophones, each on its own separate stand.

The night went on forever, visit after visit. He was beginning to understand what Melody had earlier alluded to. He still felt creepy about spying, but seeing what people were like when they were all alone with themselves was instructive. Owen confessed this to Melody as they drifted through the walls of an apartment building next to the grammar school. Again, the television was on and lit the scene of a young woman, sitting on the couch, feeding a baby with a bottle. She wore her hair in box braids and had on an orange tank top and gray sweatpants. Moving slightly forward and back as if in a rocking chair, she occasionally made noises to the child. The woman's eyes were closed and she was somewhere between the world and sleep.

"The Madonna," said Melody. She leaned over the mother to get a better look at the baby. Of course, there was no contact, but she looked at Owen and smiled. As she moved away, the glow of her arm passed over the wrist of the young woman, and he noticed a small black circle with a cross in it upon her dark skin. It was in the same spot he'd seen it on Helen's killer, and where Mrs.

Hultz said she'd spotted it on the gas station attendant. Melody pulled away but he asked her to light the area again with her arm. She did and it wasn't his imagination. They looked at it together and turned to each other.

Melody said, "What is it? What does it mean?"

Minutes later, they were outside on the street in front of the school. Melody told Owen she had to go to get up early to do some work before the day began. "See you at the bench," she said. Before he could tell her goodnight, she was gone, vanished like a light being switched off. He turned and headed home, wondering when he'd be pulled back to himself, as morning was near. He didn't bound exuberantly in his usual manner, covering a lot of ground, but walked slowly as if his experiences of the night, witnessing the lives of others, acted upon him like gravity, holding him down. He went a long way, lost to his thoughts, until something caught his attention out of the corner of his eye—a flicker of pale blue. Looking up across the street, he saw a sleeper, not Melody, standing atop the roof of a two-story house.

The person—man or woman, he couldn't tell from the distance separating them—had his/her back to him and was standing right on the ridge of the peak, leaning forward and back slightly as if shifting position as the breeze blew harder and softer. Owen was excited to see another traveler in the night world. He said nothing but walked over to the house and leaped up onto the roof, hoping the person would engage with him. As he came up behind the individual and was about to speak, he peered down into the backyard and was struck silent. There, filling and overflowing the confines of the yard, was a miasma, its yellow mist blotting out the bottom of the swing set, clothesline poles, and some small dogwood trees. It was a roiling, ever-undulating sulphur dream. He could hear it crackling and hissing.

The individual he'd approached took a step down the other side of the pitched roof. Owen watched, and as well as he could make out the details, the person was a middle-aged man. He heard the fellow praying and crying, and watched as he took two more steps on the downward slope.

"Wait!" cried Owen as it slowly dawned on him what was happening.

The man took off running the last few steps, launched himself high into the night, and as he gracefully floated toward the yellow fog, he turned in midair and looked back at whoever was behind him. There was a smile on his face as he descended, until his first contact with the miasma. It was as if he'd deluded himself into thinking this would be a painless close to a painful life. Wherever he touched it, his ethereal form turned to fizz, like the bubbles in champagne. They drifted upward and popped, amid the man's screams, which resonated throughout the neighborhood. No one in the waking world could hear. The suicide's mouth and eyes were wide with agony, and his pale blue glow flickered. He shot an arm out toward Owen, as if he'd changed his mind and suddenly wanted to live. The disintegration process drew out its work like a torturer. The clouds rolled up to envelop him, and minutes passed in torment before there was nothing left but the advancing miasma.

Owen bounded away and in his ascent was drawn back to bed.

8

OWEN WOKE TO THE memory of the man choosing to be erased from existence, and as he got out of bed, he wondered how bad life would have to be to throw it away like that. He promised himself not to think about it anymore and decided not to tell Melody what he'd witnessed.

It was Sunday, and the library wasn't open, but he went in anyway to do some research. After performing a few simple chores left over from the preceding week, Owen sat at his computer and searched for what the figure of the circle with the cross in it could possibly mean.

He found numerous variations of the image and a lot of information. In Western culture, harking back to early ancestors in the Indus River Valley, and becoming more widespread throughout Europe in the Bronze Age, the symbol stood for the power and majesty of the sun, hence it was known as the solar cross. It often adorned rulers and powerful warriors. To Native Americans of the Mound Builder culture, it represented the four directions and the sacred qualities of each. In India and China, the arms of the cross were broken and turned to create a swastika within the circle, symbolizing the cycle of life. Later, this variation was appropriated by the Nazis and came to represent death. He found the search for a specific meaning interesting, just the kind of pursuit he enjoyed, but when he was finished, he still wasn't sure what to make of it.

He *did* discover that a certain variation of the cross, where its arms extended a bit beyond the circumference of their circle, was known as the Celtic cross and widely used by Aryan hate groups. The form of the cross he was researching, the solar cross, adhered to the inner circle and was more like a wheel with spokes. There were so many variations of the design, it seemed like an idea humanity came into being with. The young woman with the baby they'd encountered the previous night made the idea of the tattoo being an Aryan hate symbol unlikely. He figured the group must have some larger purpose, but then remembered Helen on the floor behind the counter and the grim flower of her throat. That's when he gave up his search, the information he'd already found having swamped him.

In the afternoon, the rain came down harder, and since there were no patrons, for lunch he sat on the adult side and watched the downpour through the big window while eating his sandwich. It was then he hatched a plan to get Melody to go downtown with him and visit the house of the gas station attendant on Margrave Street. If he had more time before being snatched back to himself the previous night, he could have searched the woman's apartment for clues to her connection to the others marked with the tattoo. She didn't strike him as very threatening or nefarious, considering how lovingly she had held and rocked the child. He wondered what Melody would think of the plan. He'd have to explain the whole tattoo connection and about his "stakeout" with Mrs. Hultz.

Still, he was almost sure she would go with him. Although he was getting to know her a little better every night, he felt she was holding something in reserve. Perhaps she was waiting until she knew she could trust him. On the other hand, he wondered if it was that *he* was uncertain of *her*. She was spending a lot of time showing him the ropes of the night world. He had to ask himself why. She did say it was sort of her duty to help a fellow traveler. Owen doubted most people would go out of their way for a stranger, but then, maybe that was one of the lessons the night world taught.

In the afternoon, despite the umbrella, Owen got soaked heading home. Once there, he made a dinner of a bowl of Frosted Flakes and a banana. To him, cooking was burning, and things rarely turned out edible. Every two weeks, he went to the grocery store, the only time he ever used the car in his parents' garage, and he'd stop into the Chinese restaurant on the outskirts of town and have a decent meal. Otherwise, he subsisted on frozen pizza, macaroni and cheese, PB&J. Mrs. Hultz, who had him over occasionally for dinner, told him that at thirty-five, it was time to "join the adult world." Every time he thought about her saying it, he smiled—but as quickly cringed. He didn't understand what one's diet had to do with adulthood.

From the time he ate until bed, he was occupied at the kitchen table, having brought out all his boxes of magazines, the scissors, and glue. He hadn't worked on the project since the day Helen was shot. For the last few years, since he'd quit smoking, he'd been making collages from the figures and scenes of old books and magazines. The goal was a hundred collages. One for every night of a collage story to be called upon completion *100 Nights of Nothing.* He'd stolen the idea from the artist Max Ernst after receiving a collage novel at the library—*A Little Girl Dreams of Taking the Veil.* He thought the cutting of the scissors an appropriate replacement for smoking. With earphones on and classic country music crying in his skull, he toiled away. It took him months to do each page. Singing along to the songs was part of it, and a powerful concentration not even the persistence of nicotine craving could pierce. There was a story to *100 Nights,* but Owen had yet to discover what it was.

He slept and suddenly found himself on a corner in town. He had no idea why he was there or how he got there, but the wind was high and the single streetlight half a block away made it darker than if it didn't exist. He heard somebody coming from the west, dragging their feet, making slow progress. Owen worried it might be a member of the solar cross gang, coming for him. Adrenaline exploded in him and he tried to run, but his legs were too tired, as if they'd turned to stone. Instead, he backed up against the brick wall of an abandoned factory. The figure passed beneath the streetlight, an old shambling man, carrying on like a television zombie. When the stranger was upon him, he realized it was his father, or his father's corpse or ghost, and it said in an everyday tone, "This is a dream. You want to go back."

Owen woke on his back to sleep paralysis. It didn't matter how many times it happened; it was always frightening and put him in a panic until his ethereal self let go of his body and he began to rise. When he passed through the roof of his house, he immediately heard the rain. He didn't feel the cool drops, but the sound of them on leaves in the street, in puddles, sounded like music to him. The wind from the dream with his father followed him into the night world. This weather in his waking life would have drawn a scowl, but now the streetlight glistened off shimmering leaves and he found it enchanting.

By now, he was able to run without launching himself to the moon, and he bounded away to the yard with the picnic bench. His heart sank when he discovered Melody wasn't waiting for him. The rain bounced off the tabletop and he wondered how it was he could sit at the table or run along the roofs but could also pass through walls unseen and unfelt. There were shifting abilities to his perceived mass, and they seemed to be at the whim of his newly discovered state. It was still true, though, that he couldn't touch anything, and so it didn't make much sense at all. In the house behind him, a child was screaming. The parents screamed back. Owen got up and walked closer to the back door. Finally, he heard the child yell as if she was falling off a cliff, "There's a ghost in the backyard." So the spirit couldn't sneak up on him, he turned, and halfway through his spin, he realized the child was referring to him.

He passed through the hedge at the back of the property to hide. He shook his head while muttering to himself. There were so many exceptions to the rules of the night world, he wondered why there were even rules. He sat on the ground in the rain, peering through holes in the hedge, watching to see if Melody came. Eventually, after having time to think about it, he had to concede that there were just as many exceptions in the waking world. In fact, he loved those contradictions and sought them out for his reading online—Schrödinger's cat, spooky action at a distance, the double-slit electron study. These so-called "anomalies" were the loaves and fishes of his days, allowing him to believe reality had a mind of its own. An hour passed and Melody never showed. Feeling unsure, he struck out on the night's mission. It was too boring to just sit, staring through a hedge, not being able to control when he would awaken.

It was some distance downtown, so he took to the street he used to get to work—the one the Busy Bee was on—and bounded down the center of it in giant leaps that took his heels to the height of telephone poles. During one jump, he looked to his left and saw, five or six blocks away, visible even through the downpour, the yellow smudge of a miasma settling upon a rooftop, and reminded himself of all the cautions Melody had schooled him on. He stopped at the Busy Bee and stood outside its lighted window, which had been repaired. It appeared to be operating as it had before the tragedy—open all night—a young man with a ponytail behind the counter. *Amazing,* he thought, *how life and commerce go on even after such a loss.* When he left the scene, it was more like he was fleeing, escaping memories that wanted to drag him into depression. With all this on his mind, he was relieved when he finally made it to the center of town and found Margrave Street.

He no longer bounded but walked slowly, peering through the rain and the dark, trying to make out the house with the path to the front door. He recalled it was a larger piece of property than most of the others. In the night world, though, things looked different. There were two houses that could have been the place. He walked up the drive of one, passed through the front door into a darkened house. The first thing that struck him was noise coming from a back room. It sounded as if someone was being strangled. He crept down the hall, cautious, even though no one could hear him. He found the room the commotion was coming from. Passing through the door, he saw, by the glow of a night light, a young woman, naked, straddling a young man, naked, and moving frantically like a kid hyped up on sugar, riding a rocking horse. Owen put his hand in front of his face, a modesty lost to the fact that he could see through his palm.

He noticed there was a sleeper in the corner, crouched down, assiduously watching the young couple as if performing a scientific study. When Owen noticed his pale blue glow, the old man turned to him, winked, smiled, and gave a stiff mechanical thumbs-up. It wasn't that the couple having sex was devoid of any allure, but with the other sleeper there, it was too much of a reminder of the creepy nature of his home invasions. Had the old man not been there, who knows what the librarian might have done. Instead of returning the greeting, he jumped up through the ceiling and roof and landed in the front yard. He was upset with himself for becoming what he'd promised he wouldn't. Also, he realized that hadn't checked to see if the young man was the one from the gas station. He should have looked for a beard, but it wasn't what his sight had been trained on.

He moved down the street to the other place he thought might be the house of the attendant. As soon as he passed through the door, he saw the long-haired, bearded fellow sitting at a small table in the living room, the television on. In front of him was a notebook, a cup of coffee, and a silver nine-millimeter pistol. Owen walked behind the chair and looked to see what was written in the notebook. There was a list of four names, a line through three of them. The last, without a line through it and the only female name on the list, was Kiara. Owen's first thought was it could have been the woman he and Melody had visited the night before. The man wrote something next to the woman's name in a tiny, loopy script too small to make out.

Owen moved away and looked around to see what else he could find. There were local newspapers scattered on the kitchen counter. He saw the one in which the reporter called his admission that he hadn't played the hero at the Busy Bee a *confession*. Then he could see from the headlines that all of them had front-page stories about the robbery. Stuck to the refrigerator with a magnet was a photo of what looked like, as far as Owen could remember, Helen's killer. He had his arm around the shoulders of a woman holding a baby. She was definitely the young mother he and Melody had stumbled upon in the apartment building next to the school. Looking at the photo, he tried to figure out how he was going to let the police know about it. If he told them the truth, they'd send him away for psychiatric evaluation.

On the dresser in the bedroom, Owen found the stub of a paycheck from the gas station with the attendant's name on it—Aaron Feit. He mouthed the name, and just then the man entered the room, sat on the bed, and put his boots on. In the living room, he stuffed the pistol into the waist of his jeans and threw on a waterproof poncho with a hood. Then he left the house. Owen passed through the door behind him and followed him down the road, away from town.

9

A RIGHT AND A LEFT down long streets in the rain, and Feit finally stopped walking. He stepped off the sidewalk into the darker darkness beneath a stand of tall oak. With the leaves blocking some of the downpour, he pulled back his hood and took out a pack of cigarettes. The instant Owen saw them, he had an urge to smoke again.

It was obvious from where his quarry stood that Feit were there to watch the house across the street. It was a sizeable place, nearly a mansion, but so well set back amid the border of the barrens that its corner turrets and second floor with gabled roof and two dormers were lost to the passerby. The whole structure was covered in some kind of dark brown wood shake. There was light in every other window.

Feit took out his phone and made a call. The name he spoke was "Kiara." Owen moved as close as possible so as not to miss a word, and Feit partially passed through him. "I'm outside Crenshaw's now. All the lights are on. Just checking to see if there isn't another one in there with him. I can take care of him, but . . ." He listened for a time to Kiara. There was a pause. "How's William?" he asked. He nodded and hung up. Feit and Owen stood on the corner in the wind and rain, watching. Owen noticed faint classical music coming from an open window in the left-hand turret and saw shadows move throughout the rooms.

An hour later, when Feit gave up and headed away, Owen lingered on the corner. He was fairly confident either this fellow was going to rob the big old house, or he and Kiara were going to. It was obvious whoever lived there was well off. Owen stepped into the street and was crossing it before he realized he was going to pay a visit to Crenshaw. By then it had stopped raining and the wind had died down. He guessed it to be somewhere around three AM in the waking world. He swept up the long flight of front steps leading from the sidewalk and, without hesitating, passed through the door into a hallway of polished wood and a flowered runner leading him toward the inner rooms of the house.

The place was stately, with antique furniture and a lot of polished wood. The walls were covered with oil paintings and in some of the rooms, especially a darkened one, there were painted canvases in frames stacked again the walls. The pictures he passed were beautiful night scenes, stars with a gauzy glow, and pale maidens half asleep or sleepwalking yet carrying out tasks by the seashore. In one, a large canvas on the main wall of a well-lit room that appeared to be used for entertaining, there was an eerie scene of a piece of marble statuary in moonlight—a woman with flowing hair and a writhing snake around her naked waist. Then, like a cutaway, beneath the marble form, under the ground, there was a room with a satin divan. Draped across it, in an almost-awkward position, was an image of an old man, asleep. The attitude of the figure caught his eye.

Four rooms later, alternating dark and bright, he found the house's resident sitting near a blazing fireplace, its flames the only light in the room. With a long paintbrush, he was persistently dabbing a particular area with light green pigment. This painting, like the others, had a softness to the forms, as if they were beginning to disintegrate at the edges. Owen sat on the raised hearth of the fireplace, watching the old man work. At some point during his surveillance, it struck him that with all these paintings of night, this fellow might have already achieved the *100 Nights of Nothing*. He watched the artist get up and, moving slowly, go off to a kitchen somewhere and bring back a cup of tea. While sipping it, he sat quietly and stared at his progress. The classical music that had been playing in another room suddenly quit. Owen left the house, heavy with the idea he had to warn the painter that he was in the sights of the Solar Cross Gang.

As the birds began to sing—meaning sunrise was no more than an hour away—he thought that at any moment, he'd be snatched back to himself. He strode along, wrapped in thought about this supposed gang his imagination had given life to. He wondered why they would settle in Westwend. The stakes were so meager, and considering the potential danger, one would think a gang would have better plans. Crenshaw might be loaded, but the Busy Bee was a bad move, all for a weekday-morning cash drawer. There couldn't have been more than a couple of hundred dollars, most in change and small bills. Something was off. Either that or this was the laziest, dumbest gang that ever existed. Owen heard movement behind him.

When he turned, there was the old man from the corner of the first house he'd gone into on Margrave. The man approached swiftly and his hands came up in front of him. Owen detected the blank affect in the old creep's eyes. He realized this was a cord-cutter. The pale hand came toward him, aiming for his chest. Owen, surprised, spun to flee, forgetting to jump, and put one leg in front of the other. He tumbled to the ground. The cutter hovered above him and descended. Owen was on his feet in a flash, but before he could take two steps, there was another cutter directly in front of him and one coming in from the side. As the pack closed in, they made a noise like the hissing of snakes. He heard Melody's voice in the back of his mind yell, "*Jump.*"

As his three attackers converged, he flew up and away, and at the height of his ascent, he was yanked back to his earthbound body with a whooshing sound he'd never noticed before. He woke to the birdsong and the red sunrise coming through the blinds of his bedroom. A chill ran through him when the thought sank in that he almost didn't make it back. What Melody told him was true. Once you noticed the cord-cutters weren't sleepers, and you registered that frozen look in their eyes, all their actions, dictated by the screwy natural selection of the night world, elicited a sense of nausea.

Monday morning, in the children's section, he was looking for a book a mother requested. The woman followed him up and down the stacks, and her little girl, maybe three years old, followed behind her. Eventually, the book in question was found out of place in the low bookshelf that ran beneath the painting of Sleeping Beauty.

"One of the kids must have reshelved it," said Owen, and gave the book to the blond young woman who, while waiting, had lifted her daughter into her arms.

"Here's the ABCs, Jenny," the woman said to the child.

"ABCs," repeated Jenny, but paid no attention to the book. Instead, she was pointing at the mural.

"Sleeping Beauty," said Owen.

"Beard," said the child, and he laughed. The paint curling on the neck and lower chin of the fairy tale princess did resemble the shaggy beard of Aaron Feit. Upon looking at the mural, he noticed how similar the style was to the paintings in the big old house the night before. He absentmindedly handed the ABC book to the young mother, and although she thanked him, he was too preoccupied to answer. He was focused on the right-hand corner of the mural. He might have noticed before that there was a name scrawled there in tiny script, but he'd never bothered to try to decipher it. Today was different. He went to his desk and retrieved the magnifying glass he kept in the top drawer for patrons with bad sight.

Back at the mural, he leaned over and trained the glass on the signature. The name instantly became clearer. *Val Crenshaw* was how he read it, although it could have started with a sloppy H and been *Hal Crenshaw.* With this revelation, he wondered if outlandish coincidence was part of the ecosystem of the night world. His forays as a sleeper were beginning to blend with his waking life, and every evening's journey as well as every day's felt more and more like a concocted dream. The position of Sleeping Beauty in the mural matched that of the image of the man in the chamber below the marble statue, hanging in the painter's dining room. He broke from his trance and checked the book out for mother and daughter, then retired to his office and computer where he began a search for Val Crenshaw.

Along his walk home from work, Owen pondered what he'd found out. The painter was fairly well known, and had done illustration work throughout the years. When he clicked on the images associated with Crenshaw, he saw a lot of the paintings he'd run into in the old house. He also found a newspaper article someone had posted online about the mural. Valentine Crenshaw, new to Westwend, volunteered to create a picture on the wall of the children's library, which was due to open in a few months. It said in the article his one stipulation was he would have to paint it at night after his day's work. The town was thrilled with his offer. And all agreed the finished product, the Sleeping Beauty, was sublime, attracting the admiration of both children and adults.

The only problem was it stated in the article Crenshaw was twenty-eight when he did the mural in 1948. If that was accurate, it meant he was nearly one hundred years old. No doubt, Crenshaw looked old, but certainly not a century—he got around well enough to live on his own. Owen would have pegged him in his seventies. Another article listed some of the painter's more famous pieces and what they'd gone for at auction. Each painting was worth at least ten to twenty thousand dollars, and a few were a lot more. The same article mentioned museums that had bought and displayed his work. On more than one site, he was said to be an adherent of the Brandywine School of painting, centered around the artist Howard Pyle. Owen could see the influence—Crenshaw's work had the same effect of no hard lines, of obvious dry-brushing, a technique that gave a scene the look of memory.

Back home, at bedtime, he went to sleep revisiting all the coincidences and vague synchronicities of the night world, trying to sort out the actual from his own fanciful speculation. There were elusive interludes of near-solution and long whirling storms of incidents and numbers until finally, perched on the verge of an answer, he woke to the paralysis and began, again, his struggle for freedom. Equally as tantalizing as the dream, escape from the loathed state of live burial harried him for hours. At one point, he even began praying, certainly not his usual practice. And, finally, he found himself rising away from his bed and body.

As Melody approached the picnic table, Owen called to her from the other side of the hedge. She passed through and asked, "What are you doing over here?"

"A little girl who lives in the house over there saw me last night."

"Saw you? How do you mean?"

"I heard her crying to her parents there was a ghost in the backyard."

"Very rare," said Melody. "We'll have to steer clear of her."

They made their way toward the side fence and passage to the road. "What happened last night? I had to go it alone," said Owen.

"My kid was sick. He had a fever and was puking. It's going around the junior high like the Black Plague. My apologies."

Down the street, there was a house with a fake wishing well on the front lawn. It was wrapped with silk flowers. In the waking world, every day Owen passed it on the way to work, the sight made him giddy with disdain for its creepy niceness. He led Melody there and they used it as a place to sit as he filled her in on what he'd discovered the previous night. While she swung her legs, her calves disappearing through the brick work of the well top, he caught her up on the solar cross, Aaron Feit, Crenshaw, the old house, and his theory as to the caper Feit and the young mother, Kiara, had planned. He paused and added, "I think the baby's name is William."

"What a night," she said.

"And I haven't even mentioned my run-in with cutters."

"How close did they get?" She put her hand lightly to

her chest and shook her head.

"There were three of them. I tripped trying to get away and they got damn close. This one I'd seen earlier. A creepy old guy hiding in the corner of a young couple's bedroom while they were engaged in sex."

"They're known to be attracted to scenarios happening in the waking world like you mention."

"Sex?"

She nodded. "If they can't find likely sleepers to unhook, they will crowd, invisible, into the bedrooms of the living and watch as life is conceived and the silver cord is set."

"What's the chances there will be an unseen cutter around any time anyone has sex?"

"About ninety percent. And usually more than one."

"Kind of off-putting," said Owen.

"To say the least," she said.

They headed downtown, bounding down the center of the street as Owen had done the night before.

10

THE WEATHER WAS MUCH nicer that night, a soft breeze instead of a driving wind and rain. The sky was clear and the constellations looked like illustrations in a star chart. As Owen and Melody bounded along past the Busy Bee, toward the center of town, he remembered how he'd seen the miasma at a distance the previous night. When he told her, Melody said, "You were probably better off being on your own last night. Look how well you handled all of it. You need more nights like that and then I can leave you to explore alone."

"The incident with the cutters was almost fatal," he reminded her, feeling a pang that one day, she'd no longer travel the night world with him. He felt it might be too lonely to endure solo.

When they reached downtown, he showed her Margrave Street, and upon seeing the entrance to it off Cobb, the main street of Westwend, she mentioned that she once had a friend who'd lived in the house on the corner.

"What did you have in mind for when we get there?" asked Melody.

"I just wanted you to see it. Tell me what you think. Tell me how I can warn the old man, if it's not too late."

She nodded. "I agree with your assessment of what you encountered."

They reached the spot where Owen and Feit had stood the night before. Again, the lights were on in some of the rooms and music drifted out. "Barber, Adagio for Strings, Opus Three," she said.

"You're full of surprises," said Owen as they crossed the street.

"I listen to classical music all day long," she said. "It's lovely, isn't it?"

He nodded and then ascended the steps to the front door. Before he could take a breath, he and Melody were standing in the dimly lit foyer, peering down the hallway. They proceeded through the rooms. He told her that the mural adorning the wall in the children's section of the library had supposedly been painted by the old man. She stopped walking when he said it, but then quickly continued as if she didn't want him to catch her hesitation.

"What is it?" he said to her.

"Nothing really. Just sometimes, when you fall into a situation in the night world where coincidences stack up, it could be a warning of danger."

"Are you saying that about this situation?" he asked as he stopped at the entrance to the next darkened room.

"No. That's why I tried to hide my reaction to what you told me. There isn't enough of a conspiracy of reality here to warrant it. I'm offering a heads-up for the future. I don't want you to get lost in that mental morass. Stay clear. We have to help this poor guy."

When they found the old painter in the same room Owen had encountered him in the previous night, he was sitting in the same chair, holding the brush so it hovered just above the canvas. He could be perceived to be conducting the music, much sharper in the room than it had been out on the street. With his free hand he was petting a tiny black cat that lay on the arm of his chair.

"Oh, Henry," he said to the cat, gently scratched its head. "What do you think about this piece?"

The cat made a miniscule peeping sound, and Crenshaw said, "You always think I should add a small black cat. I've done five pieces with cats since you've come to stay with me." He laughed softly.

"He's adorable," said Melody.

"I'm not really a cat fan," said Owen.

"I meant the old man," she said. "The cat is too obviously adorable to have to say anything."

She walked around behind Crenshaw and watched him work as he added a moon to the nightscape he was creating. In the painting, there was a woman in a full-length white muslin dress, standing on the shoreline. Her eyes were closed, although she was facing the light of the newborn moon come to life in white, lime, and pale yellow. A few yards out in the surf, something was rising up out of the waves—an anthropomorphic form with horns and monstrous features. "It's weird but not really frightening," she said to Owen, who joined her, standing behind the artist.

"It's beautiful," he said.

She nodded.

Crenshaw had turned to some detail work on the woman's face, and was moving in with a dab of dark blue on a different brush that appeared to have but three bristles. He was just about to strike a mark of shadow on the chin when there came a loud pounding noise from the front entrance.

"My new customer," the painter said to the cat. He stood and removed the maroon robe he wore. Under it he had on a plain white shirt with the sleeves rolled up and a pair of black dress pants. He adjusted his glasses, smoothed down his sparse hair, and headed for the door. The cat leaped down from the chair arm and followed him.

"Come on," said Melody, and they followed a few feet behind the cat.

They arrived at the house's front door just as the artist was opening it. Standing there, smiling, with his hands clasped behind his back, was a young man with short hair and a dark suit and red tie. He bowed to the old man and Crenshaw invited him in. The identity of the fellow at the door wasn't clear at first, but when he laughed and introduced himself there was no doubt it was Feit, with a haircut and shave.

"That's him," he said to Melody. That's the guy I followed here last night."

"My secretary told me you prefer to do business at night," said Feit.

"Yes, come in, Mr. Feit. She told me you were interested in whatever I was working on currently. I can tell you I just added a moon to the scene. I hope you like moonglow."

"I'm excited to see it."

He led the young man down the hall and through the rooms. Along the way, Feit made admiring comments about the art on the walls and stacked in the corners. "If he threatens to kill the old man, is there something we can do?" he asked Melody.

"Nothing we wouldn't have had to prepare for well in advance. Basically, we can watch."

"I hope he lets Feit have whatever he wants."

They returned to the room with the fireplace, where the painter had been working. The music still played in the room next door, something slow and quiet from a piano. The artist showed his prospective customer to a comfortable chair a few feet away from his own painting throne. No sooner did Feit take the seat than the tiny black cat leaped into his lap. The movement startled him and his left hand moved to his inner jacket before he saw what the assault was and could quell his actions.

"I hope you're a cat fan. Henry is rather inquisitive."

"Not a problem," said Feit. "I have pets at home."

"Dogs or cats?" asked the painter.

"Cats."

"The superior beast," said the old man, who gave a knowing smile and nodded. "Stay put. Mr. Feit, I'm going to get us some tea. Do you prefer cream and sugar or plain?"

"Plain is fine."

"A perfect choice," said the host, who left through a passageway toward the back of the house to fetch the refreshments. As he disappeared through a darkened doorway, the sleepers moved around the room to get a better view of Feit. The thief tossed the cat on the floor and brushed off his pants legs with a look of disgust. He then darted a glance at the door through which the artist had retreated, reached into his jacket, and took out the handgun Owen had seen on the table at the place on Margrave Street. Feit lifted his left thigh, put the gun under it, and eased his weight back down upon it.

"You can see he's nervous," said Melody.

"That makes two of us," said Owen.

Minutes passed and the visitor put his right hand under his thigh repeatedly, no doubt practicing grabbing the gun. "Whatever is going to happen here isn't going to be good," said Melody. As she spoke, the old man came back through the doorway, pushing a silver tea cart. He poured his guest a cup and set it down on the small table next to his chair.

"Would you like a cookie?" he asked, and offered a silver tray of dainty items with frosting in a rainbow of colors.

"Forgive me, sir. I can't have sugar."

"Understood. We must have the same doctor." He set the tray down and went to sit in the chair with the easel in front of him. Once settled, he leaned forward and turned the contrivance to face his visitor so the painting was in full view.

"Oh, my. That's lovely," said Feit. "And what are you asking for it?"

"I can let you have it for eighteen thousand dollars."

"Very well." The thief put his right hand into the left-hand side of his jacket as if to withdraw his wallet, but at the same time, Melody pointed out to Owen that Feit was reaching for the gun with his left hand. Even though they knew full well the gun was in the offing, they were

Jeffrey Ford

both shocked when they saw it rise up. Both looked to
Crenshaw. In an instant, the old man's face went through
a remarkable transformation, from the kindly old painter
to a beetle-browed demon. The sleepers stepped back in
shock. Feit aimed, but before he could pull the trigger,
the artist pounced with a vicious growl. It happened so
fast, neither Owen nor Melody could more than barely
register it. As the gun went off, Crenshaw, having leaped
in a blur, was on his prey, pushing away the weapon. The
shot went wide and high into the ceiling as Feit's throat
was ripped out by the old man's teeth in a gush of blood
and a rapidly drowning cry of agony.

Melody froze but Owen screamed, loud and shrill.
Crenshaw, who was lapping at the gaping throat while
Feit's body jerked and shuddered, suddenly spun around
as if he could hear the cry. His glistening green eyes
searched the shadows and glanced about the room as he
sniffed the air. "He heard me," said Owen.

"Back up," whispered Melody. "Just keep backing up
till we're through the wall."

The creature that had been the painter stood and
started in their direction, his clawed hands out in front
of him. The sleepers stepped back and back and passed
through the wall into another room. It was a large bathroom with red tile on the floor and walls. A woman, obviously dead, hung upside down, her long hair reaching

down into the tub of blood beneath her.

"God. What is this?"

"Just keep going till we're on the street," said Melody.

They pushed through a number of other rooms that smelled like a slaughterhouse, but neither of them stopped to look around. Eventually, they drifted to the ground on the side of the house and bounded away into the night.

11

THEY SAT ON SWINGS next to each other in the children's playground behind the baseball diamond at the park. The night was still, whatever breeze there had been before now gone. The only sound, spring creepers and an owl. It was late enough that no traffic passed on the road a quarter of a mile away.

"What the hell?" said Owen.

"*What the hell* is right," said Melody. "That was horrifying."

"Did you know about this? Modern vampires in Westwend?" he asked. "Gangs and cutters and the miasma, people tripping on cicada-ass fungus? And now vampires?"

"I've never encountered it before," she said.

"Had you ever heard of it in your travels?"

"Only rumors that sounded so outlandish, I passed them off as mere traveler's tales. Exaggerations about an already-astonishing realm."

"I think we can rule this one legit."

"There's so much going on at night, in the shadows, that people who spend most of their waking time in the sunlight have no idea about. Neon and spotlights and bulbs have pushed back the darkness, but night is still largely an undiscovered territory."

"I thought vampires didn't like cats."

"Owen, please, this isn't a Bela Lugosi flick. This is the real thing. We're calling him a vampire, but he may be something else entirely. And he probably doesn't adhere to the rules of fiction—wooden stakes and garlic, the lack of a reflection in mirrors."

"He has the bloodletting thing down fairly well."

"I wouldn't take anything for granted."

"And he heard me. That girl saw me in her backyard, the dog saw me in that couple's bedroom a few nights ago, and the vampire heard me. What is it about me? I'm the least stealthy sleeper in town."

"Creatures like this might have the extrasensory abilities of a dog or gifted child. Perhaps they sense you more readily because you don't really belong here. I don't think he saw us, but he obviously knew we were there. We're dangerous to him and he'll come looking for us."

"I doubt anyone would believe us about him—especially not the cops."

"We don't have to convince them he's a vampire. We just have to interest them in going inside his place to look for that dead girl's body and the remains, if there are any, of Feit."

"Do you think he was there to rob Crenshaw, or was he really there to kill him, knowing he was a vampire?" asked Owen.

"I'm confused. I could believe he was there to assassinate the old man if not for the fact his tattooed compatriot shot up the convenience store and murdered your friend's daughter."

"Yeah, that makes no sense. There is one person who might know, though."

"Kiara?"

He nodded. "But how do I broach the subject, and if I manage to, what are the chances she won't shoot me?"

"It's either that or we go to the police, I guess," said Melody. "One thing's for sure: I bet he'll come looking for us in the night world."

"How will he know it's us?"

"Did you see him sniff the air?"

"How can there be an odor if there's no body? It doesn't make sense."

"Maybe our ethereal forms have some kind of signature scent for him."

"This sleeper business was altogether wonderful and magical before tonight. Now it's altogether horrible."

"Well, we could decide not to travel at night, but you're not capable of controlling your abilities like I can," she said.

"Melody, I feel it coming on. I feel the vibration in

my chest from when I get . . ." Owen was pulled back to himself.

The next day, instead of walking, Owen drove the car to work for the first time in recent memory. Once he got there, he hid out in his office and showed himself only when he had to check books out for the patrons, which, thankfully, were few. Even the dozen or so he helped, he eyed suspiciously, although he'd known most of them since they were born. He was put off by the younger Kelsey boy's incisors and Mrs. Morton's selection of *Interview with the Vampire*. Throughout the day, he was undecided about visiting Kiara. He had to tell her about Feit and desperately wanted to know what she knew. His other consideration was whether to buy a gun or see if he could borrow Mrs. Hultz's husband's.

In the afternoon, he researched news stories of missing persons last seen in or who lived in Westwend. As best as he could ascertain, there had been zero going back at least two decades. But then he was sorry he looked, because in searching for "missing persons" in the county, the hits started accruing from nearby towns. The phenomenon was fairly frequent, but consciously, carefully dispersed in a sixty-mile radius, going back to the 1960s. People did sometimes leave town, though. Because no one knew where they went didn't necessarily mean they'd been abducted, killed, and drained by a vampire.

Owen counted twenty-five, and those were the ones local police knew about. Granted, they were spread out over eight towns and four times as many years. The police departments in those towns by the barrens were understaffed, and the crime rate for drug-related offenses had risen in the 1990s, taking a good portion of those departments' resources and time. Old Crenshaw was a crafty individual. He killed like a rabid dog but had the acumen of a tactician. If he killed a person every so often, he could drain them into his tub and save the blood somehow—if he could prevent it from clotting—to ingest over time.

At the end of the workday, Owen closed the library and drove to the apartment building located across a field next to the grade school. The building held only six apartments, split evenly between two floors. He remembered that Kiara's rooms were on the second floor. Parking in front of the place, he sat for a few minutes, weighing his decision to contact her. Revealing that he had secret information on Feit that could only have been gathered through spying might not sit well with the gang. Also, she might not believe him as to what happened and blame Owen for her friend's death. "How many people would believe me?" he wondered. Still, he turned the car off, opened the door, and got out. He wasn't sure if it was the sight of the blood or the primal sound the creature made in its attack, but he felt unsafe and didn't like being out in the open.

He found her name on the mailbox downstairs—K. BOLDEN, APT #6. There was no security, so he had no problem simply walking up to the second floor, heading down the hallway to its end, and finding her door. He took a deep breath, exhaled, and knocked, lightly at first before realizing no one would hear him. He considered running away and then knocked louder. A few moments passed without response, although he eventually noticed there was music playing inside. He was about to knock again when a female voice answered. "Who is it?"

"Owen Hapstead," he said, and then nervously added, "I'm the town librarian," which he immediately regretted.

"We don't have any books out and don't use the library."

"Yes, ma'am, I know. I have information for you about Aaron Feit." This statement was met with silence. "He's an acquaintance of yours, is he not?" He stood waiting for a half minute before there finally came a response.

"Hold on," said the voice. A little more time passed and then he could hear the chain lock sliding off. The deadbolt clicked, and the door swung back. "Come in," she said, but he couldn't see where she was. He took a tentative step through the threshold, and the instant he was inside, the door slammed shut behind him, a forearm came up and wedged into his throat. There was something hard and pointed jabbed into his back. He saw in front of him, the baby, William, sitting in a high chair near a table in the kitchenette across the apartment.

"Who sent you?" she said.

"Nobody; I've come to tell you something tragic has befallen your colleague."

"Colleague?"

"The tattoo you all share."

"What about Aaron?"

"I hate to tell you this, but he was attacked and killed."

"By who?"

"I'm not trying to be obtuse, but the question is more *by what* than *who.*"

"What's that supposed to mean?"

"Do you believe in vampires?" he asked.

She didn't answer but he felt the gun withdraw from his back and her forearm drop away, leaving him able to breathe properly again.

"Thank you," he said.

"You're not a cop?"

"I told you, I'm the librarian."

She gave him a shove toward the kitchenette. "Sit down."

Owen took a seat and held his hands up as if to calm

her. "I know how strange this is," he said.

She sat across from him next to the high chair but kept the gun trained on him. With her free hand she lifted a small bowl of dry Cheerios off the table and dumped a little pile of them onto William's tray. The toddler saw them, smiled, and blew a few bubbles. He pressed his index finger into the hole on one of the bits of cereal and it stuck. Then he lifted it to his mouth.

"Start talking," said Kiara.

"First, a question," said Owen.

She cocked the pistol, and he automatically brought his hands up in front of his face. "No, I need to know this so I can tell you the right thing."

"Go ahead," she said, carefully released the hammer, and laid the gun on the table in front of her.

"Was Feit at the old man's house to rob him or to assassinate him?"

"To kill him before he could kill anyone else."

"You know he's a vampire or something like that?"

Kiara nodded. "He killed my husband."

"Wait, the man who held up the Busy Bee?"

"Crenshaw bit him and put him under some kind of mind control. He was directed to hold up the store. He knew Duane was part of our organization and that we were closing in on him. It was a warning to put us off and to put the police on our trail. He's powerful."

"You all have the solar cross tattoo," he said. "I looked it up."

"Right."

"Why that?"

"These creatures, we call them Ambrogio, from an ancient tale, don't operate well in the sun. They don't burn up like in the movies, but sunlight stuns them and makes them much more vulnerable. Daylight short-circuits their nervous systems. Now . . . Aaron."

"My friend and I saw Aaron get attacked by Crenshaw. It was horrible. His throat was torn out. Your partner got a shot off but that was it. The old man moved too quickly."

She closed her eyes and fell back into her chair with a heavy sigh. Tears leaked from beneath her eyelids. "I told him not to go alone." Owen kept his mouth shut, allowing her to grieve. A couple of minutes passed in silence before she wiped her eyes and cheeks with the backs of her hands and sat forward again.

"This is the part that's hard to believe." He was surprised she didn't stop him in the middle of his lengthy explanation. When he asked her if she knew what an OBE was, she nodded confidently. She also knew about traveling in the night world, and informed him that the Ambrogio traveled in sleep as well, but took to their beds during the day.

"You mean that thing could be at large in Westwend right now? Invisible?"

"He could be right in this room, listening to us," she said. "That's why it was so goddamn stupid of you to come here."

Owen was stunned. He turned around as if he might see the old man materializing in the corner. "Can he hurt me when in his ethereal form?"

"I don't think so."

"Can you kill him?"

"I have special bullets that explode in the body and release phosphorous. All I have to do is get one in him anywhere from head to toes."

"What are we gonna do?"

She took out her cell phone and whispered, "Give me your number."

He whispered it back, even though he knew, if Crenshaw was in the room with them, he'd have it.

"I need someone to watch my son while I'm out hunting," said Kiara.

"I might have someone for you," he said. "I'll text you later. Are you going after him by yourself?"

"No, you're going to help me."

12

OWEN WAS SWEATING BY the time he left Kiara's apartment. He couldn't get it out of his mind that the spirit presence of the old man could be trailing him, bounding along behind his car, seeing everything, peering into their preliminary plans. He stopped at the market on the way home in order to buy something easy to make for dinner. His scheme was to invite Mrs. Hultz over to eat and, in the process, try to talk her into babysitting William and lending him her husband's gun. It was amazing to him that with so much on his mind, he could still be so devious. When he got out of the car and walked across the market parking lot, the feel of the persistent wind against his face made him think of a wispy Crenshaw swirling around him.

He chose pork chops for dinner. Also asparagus. The checkout lines were long because only two aisles were open. While he was waiting, a family passed by—two kids, a girl of about twelve and a boy, perhaps fourteen. The father, gaze on the ground, hands in his pockets, had raven-black hair and seemed in a dark mood. The mother exuded a kind of energy and looked familiar to Owen. Then he realized he was seeing Melody in the waking world. Definitely middle-aged, but tall and solidly put together, mid-length hair going gray. Her face wasn't in an open smile, but she seemed calm and content. She turned and said something to her husband, who laughed and put his arm around her. As they passed from his sight, Owen was surprised that he felt something nebulously akin to jealousy.

Later, after having burnt the pork chops beyond recognition and boiled the asparagus to mush, he ordered a pizza and took it next door. He knocked but there was no answer. The inside door was open, and although the screen was closed, he found it wasn't latched. After calling "Hello" numerous times and getting no answer, he pushed open the door and entered. From the foyer, looking across the lavender living room, he saw Mrs. Hultz slouched in the chair. He wondered, with a shiver, if the vampire artist somehow found out she was a tangential but important part of the plan and had done her in. As he was bolting toward her chair, he heard her snore. She opened her eyes as he stood over her and said, "Is this a nightmare?"

"No," he told her, "the nightmare is next door. Burnt pork chops and overcooked asparagus. I was making dinner for you. How about pizza?"

She pulled herself up in the chair and, blinking her eyes, said, "That sounds swell."

Mrs. Hultz insisted on having hers with gin, but Owen had read somewhere that alcohol makes you sleep poorly, and he had to make it to the night world later. They sat in the living room with dinner trays set up in front of them. On the TV was an old black-and-white crime movie with Jack Palance called *House of Numbers*. He wanted to spring the question on her about babysitting before she had too much to drink.

"How are things going for you, Owen?" she asked.

"Well," he said. "Better, but there's only one problem."

"Tell me," she said.

"I have a date tonight but it's contingent on whether I can find a babysitter for my girlfriend's son."

"A date?

"Yeah."

She clapped and the bracelets on her wrists jangled. "What about the old woman who's your neighbor?"

"I never thought of it," he said.

"I've gotten so easy in my old age. Sold out for a pizza," she said.

"You will?"

She nodded. "I'd better stop drinking. Tell your friend to bring the child over at seven; we can spend a half hour getting acquainted."

"I have one other favor to ask you."

"What now?"

"I was wondering if you could show me your husband's gun. You know, the gat."

"Why?"

He was taken aback, and grasped at the first lie he could think of. "I have a friend who trades in old guns. He told me that a lot of times, they don't have to be all that old and people usually don't know their value. In other words, you could be sitting on a mint."

"A mint? Please. For that old peashooter?"

He thought his ploy had failed, but after Mrs. Hultz had finished the slice of pizza she was working on, she got up and went into the dining room. He watched her go to a hutch and open a waist-high middle drawer. From it she retrieved a revolver. She closed the drawer with her hip and grasped the gun by the handle. "I'll fill you full of lead," she said, the gun wobbling in her unsteady grip.

"Do you have bullets for it?"

"It's loaded right now."

"Loaded," he yelled. "Don't point it at me." He squirmed in his chair and it reminded him of Helen at the Busy Bee when she first faced the gunman's weapon.

"Don't be such a wimp," she said, and handed the gun over to him. "I think it's a Colt .38 Special. Some cops in the thirties carried them. I don't know where Stan got it."

"OK," said Owen, "I just wanted to see it. I'll tell my friend and ask what he thinks it's worth."

Mrs. Hultz walked back into the dining room. "I don't know if I'd ever sell it," she said. "You know, sentimental value." She returned the gun to the middle drawer. A little while later, when she got up to go to the bathroom, Owen went to the hutch, opened the drawer, and carefully put the gun into his jacket pocket. When Mrs. Hultz returned to the living room, she grilled him on her babysitting assignment. He told her his friend Kiara would bring the baby over to her house, which would make it easier. She said that was fine.

"Tell her to remember some of the child's toys and a blanket, and if she has a fold-down crib for him to sleep in, that would be great," said Mrs. Hultz.

"Got it," said Owen, and then washed the plates and glasses they'd used while she cleaned up and put the leftover pizza in the refrigerator. Soon after, he went back to his place, where he texted Kiara and told her he'd secured a babysitter. He gave her his address and told her he'd lifted the gun from Mrs. Hultz. She wrote back that she'd be over in about an hour, and then added, "Don't shoot yourself." He was, at first, surprised by her sense of humor, but then it came to him she might not be kidding. Looking at the gun he'd laid on his kitchen table, he saw the muzzle pointed directly at him. With his pinky finger, he slowly spun the business end of the weapon away.

As he sat musing about Crenshaw and Kiara and Mrs. Hultz, something nagged at him. The entire situation was, in fact, ridiculous. A vampire? A vampire painter, no less. Running around after dark in the guise of a disembodied spirit, interceding in some age-old power struggle between good and evil. All that was swirling in his thoughts, but the one thing foremost on his mind was Melody. He didn't think it was fair involving her. It was too dangerous and only a matter of time before the old man figured out who his invisible guests were. Perhaps he already knew. She had twice as much to lose, seeing as she was married and had children. He hoped to see her that night and talk her out of participating in whatever plan he and Kiara could stir up.

The sun had nearly set when Kiara showed up at his door with William in her arms. She was frowning and the baby was smiling. She was wearing all black: tight black jeans, a black T-shirt, athletic shoes, and a concealed-carry tactical bag slung across her back. He let her in and they sat at the table in the kitchen. He made her coffee but he had warm milk, hoping it would make him drowsy so he'd fall asleep quicker. She put the toddler down and he waddled off into the living room with his puppy doll and plopped down on the carpet. "Got any ideas?" asked Owen.

Kiara nodded. She pulled out her phone and signaled she was going to text him. Crenshaw could be spying on them from his own OBE. Owen turned his screen on and waited while she typed, her fingers moving in a blur over the tiny keyboard. A few seconds later, there was a *ding* and he looked down. The message read, When you achieve night world, go to the painter's and find him. Look for best way in. Once night comes, we can bet he'll be awake, so no worries that he'll be in the night world. I need to take him by surprise.

Owen nodded to show he understood, then typed, How will I communicate with you?

Leave phone on, volume turned up, she wrote. I'll call and wake you before going in and you can give me the info. We'll set a time. Midnight.

1, he texted back.

She nodded her agreement.

If I haven't traveled, he wrote, don't enter the house. He's fast and vicious.

"OK," she said aloud, putting down her phone. She then picked up Mrs. Hultz's gun from the table. Grabbing it by the handle, she aimed it away from them and unlatched the cylinder. With her free hand, she pushed the cylinder through the frame to reveal all the chambers.

She squinted, then latched it closed. "You've only got two bullets in here," she said.

Owen nodded like he knew it all along, and she shook her head.

"Don't put your finger on the trigger until you see what it is you're going to shoot. You don't want to misfire with only two bullets. With these rounds, you can hurt him and stop him for a minute or two. That's all the time it'll buy you. I doubt you'll have to use it, but if you do, aim for the heart or the head. The heart of the Ambrogio is dead center." She pointed directly at her solar plexus.

Owen and Kiara took William next door to Mrs. Hultz's house, along with his paraphernalia of playpen and bottles and blankets. The old lady was, of course, as Owen had expected, nearly unbearable. Taking William in her arms, she led Kiara around the dining room, where all her photos were on the hutch and the wall surrounding it. "I have three children, all daughters," she said. "All grown and married." Owen guessed she took the young mother on a tour of her family in order to illustrate there was nothing to worry about, her baby was in good hands. That wasn't enough, though. She went on to point out the photos of Owen when he was a baby and in grade school, high school, et cetera. "He was cute," said his neighbor.

"I've always gone for the pale, nerdy types," said Kiara.

"Well, you hit paydirt with this one," said Mrs. Hultz.

Owen could feel himself blushing.

"We have to get going," he said.

Kiara ran through her nightly routine with William. Mrs. Hultz nodded and said, "Everything will be fine, dear. Go and have a wonderful time. Don't worry if you get back late; you can always pick him up in the morning. He can sleep in his playpen. I'll watch him like a hawk."

As they walked next door, Owen said, "The pale, nerdy ones?"

For the first time, he heard Kiara laugh out loud. They wished each other good luck. He quietly slipped into his house and, without turning on the lights, headed for the bedroom. Outside he heard two car doors open and close. He smiled, knowing Kiara was working to throw Mrs. Hultz off from suspecting anything amiss. As the vehicle pulled away, he laid his head upon the pillow, closed his eyes, and tried to think of anything but the old man's bloody maw.

13

WHEN HE AWOKE IN a state of paralysis, he struggled to turn and see the clock on his nightstand, but, of course, he was unable to move so much as a toe. He gained control of himself by deep breathing and concentrating on those counting on him. It took quite a while, but eventually he achieved release from his body and floated up and out onto the street. The night had changed since he'd been at Mrs. Hultz's place with Kiara. There was a thick fog infused with scattered streetlight glow, and the night world looked more magical and more frightening than he'd yet experienced it. The thought came to him before he headed in the direction of the meet-up spot with Melody that they'd again have to enter the lair of the Ambrogio.

His nerves settled somewhat when he saw, through the holes in the hedge, the pale blue form of Melody. Instead of leaping over the shrubs from next to the picnic table, he passed through it. She was standing with arms folded, staring up through the fog as if trying to see the moon. "Back to hell?" she asked. Owen told her the plan and she nodded. "Sounds reasonable. And the woman, Kiara, has the means to kill it?"

"She has a gun that shoots bullets with phosphorous. What phosphorous has to do with it, I have no idea."

"The ammunition probably bursts into flames when it strikes."

They left the backyard and bounded down the street toward the center of town. The pace and height of their jumps was almost perfectly synchronized. "I found something out you're not going to like any better than I do," she said.

"What now?" said Owen. "I'm already shaking."

"These creatures have the ability to sever one's silver cord when in the night-world state."

"Wait," said Owen, and landed on the sidewalk across the street from the Busy Bee. "What the hell?"

"That's what my teacher told me," said Melody.

"Who's this teacher of yours?"

"A very old woman. She's an experienced traveler who has encountered almost every possible circumstance one can in the night world. She's taught me about traveling the night world since my original teacher passed away."

"Did she happen to have any possible weapons or defenses against the old man?"

"There's only one other thing that might buy us a little more time or space. There's a way to exert minimal physical force by gathering energy from the ethereal form."

"What's that mean?"

"If I concentrated, I could actually push Crenshaw away. I wouldn't have the ability to hurt him, but merely to repel him. It drains an alarming amount of energy, though. I might still have the ability to bound away, but I wouldn't be very swift."

"Well, let's hope he's awake and not waiting for us in the night world. Could the physical force you emanate in your invisible form repel him in his physical form?"

They began traveling again. "Yes," she said. "But it would be a weaker push than if both he and I were in the night world."

"How is it done?"

"It's too complicated for me to show you now. There's a sophisticated string of imagery you focus on. You sort of have to charge up, like you're revving an engine, then push outward with all your might."

There was silence on the remainder of the journey down Margrave, past Feit's old place, and along the two streets and their turns beyond it. They stood beneath the stand of oaks across the street from the house. The windows were completely dark, save for one light on in a third-floor window.

"Chilling," said Owen. "I know this has nothing to do with dreams, but I've never been engaged in anything more nightmarish in my life. When I really think about it, the entire thing is madness."

"I'm leery of it too," said Melody, "but if we ignore it, it's not going to go away."

"But you have kids, and young kids at that."

"How do you know how old my kids are?"

"I saw you in the market with your family."

"I wish you hadn't," she said. "I like to keep separate my night travels and my waking life."

"I understand. I was going to suggest that you leave this to me."

"I can't now. I've taken you on as a pupil."

"Not to be grim, but I just don't want to imagine your husband waking up one morning and finding your lifeless body next to him. That scares me more than this dark house."

"Why?"

"It would be terrible for your children, for your partner. I care about you."

"You do?"

"I do, and if you know me, that's not like me at all. I'm pretty much a loner. I usually care more about a book out of place at the library than any person."

She smiled. "I'll keep it in mind. Now, come on, we only have an hour before Kiara is going to call and wake you."

"Shit," Owen whispered, and they started across the street.

They huddled inside the foyer, in the dark, for a few long minutes, listening to the creaks and pops of the big old house. There was no music playing. They knew the predator would be wary and somehow, to some extent, he could hear and smell them.

"Should we try upstairs first? If he's up there, we can then look for a way for Kiara to get in down here."

"It could be a trap, though. He's as sly as the devil himself."

"Maybe, but we might as well rule it out."

"Do you recall seeing a stairway anywhere?"

As they spoke, they crept down the hallway. In every room, they encountered a night-light plugged into an outlet near the floor. That was enough to see most of a room, but anything could have been lurking in the deep shadows of the opposite corner. Owen's stomach muscles trembled and the hairs on the back of his invisible neck were at attention. He was about to leap right up through three floors and out of the place. If he actually saw the painter come lunging out of the dark, growling, it would probably be startling enough to wake him into his body. If not, he'd certainly be finished. Melody, who led the way, was only a little braver than Owen, keeping her hands out in front of her like a kid playing Marco Polo.

They turned in a direction they'd not gone the previous night and discovered the stairs. "Let's split up," she said. "I'll take the upper floors; you try the basement."

"Underground?" said Owen.

"OK, I'll take the basement."

He shook his head and started up the stairs. She was moving toward the back of the house, and he called after her, "Psst. Where will we meet?"

"Outside, across the street. In a half hour."

He ascended, mumbling to himself. On the second floor, there were rooms off the hallway. Again, paintings lined the wall. Owen found them enchanting, much like a fairy tale vision, and he admonished himself for doing so. The old man was a serial killer proffering romantic scenes of pale beauties in the moonlight. Tiptoeing along the thick carpet, although there was no reason to, he poked his head into each room. Nothing in the décor said *vampire.* Two were bedrooms and one was a study with wooden bookcases set into all the walls, save for a window and the door. Owen's fear left him, and he wanted to go through the room and see what was on the shelves. Many of the volumes looked ancient and rare.

He stopped in the bathroom at the end of the hall and rested on the closed toilet lid. He listened intently and heard a faint sound coming from upstairs. He noticed an extra roll of toilet paper kept in a yellow crocheted hat exactly like the one his grandmother had in her bathroom. He got up, passed through the door, and headed for the stairs to the top floor. As he climbed, he heard a murmuring sound that grew more pronounced as he went. Again, on the third floor there was a hallway with a number of rooms off it. When he made it to the landing, he saw a light shining through a partially open door. It looked to be the room they'd noticed from the street.

He crept up to the open door and peered in. The old man was inside doing something. He could only see him from the back. He was leaning over, maybe painting on a flat desk instead of the easel. Owen stepped through the door. The sight of a body lying on a rolling gurney came into view. He drew slowly closer and saw it was a young man, his stomach split wide open and the flaps of flesh folded back to his sides. Organs and entrails glistened in the bright overhead light. Crenshaw was dipping a paintbrush into the gore of the gaping wound.

Owen turned, unable to look anymore, and staggered away. He could barely stay on his feet. Before he could flee, he realized what the murmuring was. The young man on the gurney was still alive, his eyes wide and glassy, his mouth moving ever so slightly and sound coming from it. It was as if he was trying to discuss with himself what the hell had happened to him. The librarian groaned, and when he did, he saw Crenshaw spin around and look toward the door where he stood. The painter stared directly at him. Owen froze and waited, trying to escape detection. The victim then groaned in a weaker voice, much the way Owen had, and the painter turned back to his infernal work.

He flew down the stairs in two long jumps from landing to landing. When he hit the main floor, he passed through walls and furniture, cutting straight to the front of the house and out onto the street. He made for the stand of oaks and stood in its deep shadow, shivering. There was no doubt in his mind that they had to try to kill this monster. A few minutes later, he saw Melody emerge from the side of the place. She bounded across the street and joined him.

"There are bodies in the basement, dried out, almost crystalized, hanging from the ceiling on steel hooks like tobacco curing. I wasn't sure at first if they were human. He's drying them out like beef jerky," she said.

"How many?"

"A half dozen. There are also vats of blood simmering at a low boil and being slowly syphoned into bottles a drip at a time. There's a walk-in freezer, frost on the walls, where he stores the bottles. It's like his own little blood factory."

"Is there any place for Kiara to get in?"

"Yes, there's an unlatched window in a window well at

the back of the house. She just has to push it open and ease herself down."

"He's upstairs painting with blood and guts. He's got some guy on the verge of death with his stomach split open, and he's dabbing a paintbrush in him. If I had my body with me, I'd have vomited. He was so intent on his work, it was almost ridiculous; the nonchalance. No matter how we hurry to get help, that guy on the table isn't coming back."

"It reeks of death a hundred times over down in the basement."

"I hope Kiara shows up soon."

While they stood there waiting, they tried to lean into each other to find comfort from the horror. He reached up and put an arm around Melody but it passed right through her. It must have been around one AM when they saw a car come up the street and pull over on the wooded side five or six houses down. Someone got out of the car and came toward their spot.

He could tell by the silhouette of her braids in the light from the streetlamp and her trim figure it was Kiara. "Here we go," he said.

"I'm going to stay beside her and see if I can help in some way," said Melody.

Owen was going to answer, but by then, Kiara had taken out her cell phone and dialed his number. He was reeled into his body and he instantly heard his cell phone ringing next to him on the night stand. He answered it. She spoke in a whisper. "What did you see?" she said.

"He was in the attic. Melody says there's an unlatched window in a window well at the back of the house. You just have to find it and push it open. Let yourself in."

"Got it," she said.

"Be careful," he called out, but she'd already hung up. He pictured her taking the long-barreled revolver with the phosphorous shells out of the bag that hung across her shoulder. When she had the gun in hand, she slung the bag across her back, pointed the weapon upward, and glided across the street with stealth and grace. The image of her cleared from his mind, and he headed for the kitchen to see if there was another bottle of bourbon squirreled away anywhere.

14

HE WAS SOMEWHERE INTO his second drink when his phone, lying on the kitchen table, rang. It was so unexpected, he nearly jumped out of his chair. He scooped it up, dropped it, and grabbed it again.

"Kiara?" he said into it.

"It's Melody. I just woke myself in order to tell you, Crenshaw was waiting for her in the basement. It looks to have been a trap. She's still alive, beat up and locked in that cold room. He's got her gun. I can't talk anymore." The phone went dead.

In gym shorts and T-shirt, Owen slipped on his sneakers and grabbed Mrs. Hultz's gun. He was in the garage, in the car, and starting it in less than a minute. His heart was pounding as he tried desperately to figure out what to do. He was a librarian, not a vampire assassin like the members of the solar cross. He whispered more curse words in the quick drive than he'd uttered in his entire life. When he got close to the house, he turned off the lights and coasted as quietly as possible behind Kiara's car. Slipping out of the front seat, he eased the door closed and headed up the street. His respiration was fast and shallow.

He knew there was nothing he could do but blunder in through the basement window and hope the old man might have gone elsewhere. It was pitch black behind the house. Stumbling, and once falling to his knees, he nearly discharged one of his two bullets and lost the element of surprise. After tripping twice, he turned on the flashlight app of his phone. When it first lit the night, it shone on a white figure standing back in the yard amid a semicircle of birch trees, a naked woman with a snake around her waist. The form frightened him and he turned back to the house. He finally found the right window, took a deep breath, and let himself in. He gagged. Melody had been right; it stank like chopped meat gone bad, but on a supernatural level. "God," he whispered to himself, and put the phone away so as not to give any warning. Lifting the gun, he peered through the dim light to get his bearings.

He headed down a short hallway with a red light at the end of it. Crouched over in an attempt to make himself inconspicuous, he kept his right side to the wall. Every few feet, he stopped and listened carefully. At its end, the hallway opened into a large room lit in red like some scene out of Hell. He saw the vats of blood Melody had mentioned, and the dried-out corpses hung from hooks. It was still too dim to see well, so he felt around the walls for the door to the cold room. Eventually, his hand passed over the doorknob. Trying it, he found the room unlocked. He pulled the door back a sliver. Thinking at first the sound that rose up to be the squeal of the hinges, he quickly realized the noise came from upstairs—an animal sound like a wolf or coyote on the hunt. Growling followed it and he knew Crenshaw was on to him. His gun hand started to tremble.

It was freezing in the room and there was only the dim red light shining in through the open door. What initially looked like a duffel bag leaning against the wall stirred. It exhaled a cloud of steam and staggered upright. It was Kiara. He pulled out his phone and pressed the flashlight app. In the glare from it he saw she had a wicked bump and bruise on the side of her face. "My gun is gone," she whispered.

He heard the Ambrogio pounding down the stairs at top speed. Stuffing the phone back in his pocket, Owen said, "He's coming." She made it to his side and they got clear of the freezer just as a blur moved quickly through the red light. Lifting his gun, he pulled the trigger, but the hammer fell on an empty chamber. Kiara pulled him down to his knees at the last second as a clawed hand swept over their heads.

Owen aimed and pulled the trigger again. There was the click of another empty chamber, nearly bringing tears to his eyes. Then one more time, just as the creature was upon them. A small explosion and the force of the slug stopped the artist in his tracks. He stood up straight in front of them, and Kiara sprang to her feet. On the ascent, she dealt the predator a stiff right to his jaw and a kick to the side of the head. He teetered backward and splashed into a vat of blood. Kiara grabbed Owen's hand and they fled up the stairs from the basement. How he wished he could bound right out of the house as he could when traveling the night world. They searched frantically for the hallway on the main floor. When they found it, she worked the chain locks and dead bolts to open the front door while he stood back to back with her, the gun up, its single bullet ready to fire.

As Crenshaw reached the main floor, he bellowed, and it was then that Kiara cleared the last lock and flung the door open, and both of them sprinted toward their cars. She told him to meet her at the baseball diamond in the park, which had been a meet-up point they'd discussed. He just had enough time to say OK before she'd leaped into her car and hit the gas. He wished he'd moved faster. Her pulling away left him with a desolate feeling. He got into his own ride and hit the gas. There was no sign of Crenshaw. The birds were singing in full chorus. Sunrise was on its way.

They sat side by side in the bleacher seats, the way he and Melody had the previous night, looking out across the baseball diamond. Owen still held Mrs. Hultz's gun at the ready. Kiara shook her head and said, "He moved so fast when he first came at me in the basement, I didn't have a chance to even get a shot off. He put me down with one punch and locked me in the freezer, no doubt for later feeding. It's a disgrace. I should have been able to do something."

"Listen," he said, "I saw firsthand what he did to Feit. I'm surprised you went in there after him. Also, that kick you laid on him was like something out of a movie."

"The question is, what now?" she said.

"I'm out of ideas. Maybe we should just call the cops and let them handle it. I know a lot of the town's officers. I could say I was bringing some books to a patron of the library who was laid up, but I went to the wrong house, went in, and saw a dead body. I'm pretty sure they'd check it out."

"Nah," she said. "I have to get a better weapon, and I've got a small flamethrower back at my apartment. If we send the cops in there, think how many will be killed."

"Wait," said Owen, "a flamethrower and dead cops? This whole thing is way beyond my abilities. I'm a small-town librarian on the edge of the pine barrens."

"You're in it now. He's seen us and will be looking for us."

"OK, we'll have to come up with something."

"Good," she said. "That'll keep you alert. Now, here's what we should tell Mrs. Hultz."

He left the baseball field first and drove home. He'd left the garage open so he could scoot quickly into it without Mrs. Hultz realizing he and Kiara had left in separate cars last night. She arrived in her car two minutes after he'd left the garage. As they walked up the path toward Mrs. Hultz's front door, the old woman opened it. She held the child wrapped in a blanket and was smiling with sleepy eyes.

"He slept great," she said. "But I stayed up all night just watching him. It's been so long since my own were that new."

Kiara wove a smooth tale around their having been out all night and their trials and tribulations. By the time he left to go next door, Mrs. Hultz had acquiesced to watch William for two more nights. Kiara added a stack of cash to sweeten the deal. Owen walked her and William to her car. She told him, "I have to kill this fuckin' thing now, or it's ultimately going to take my kid."

"What do you have in mind?" he asked.

"I'm going to hunt him down wherever he is and burn him to a cinder."

"I'll be here later, after work; come and get me."

In the hour he had left to sleep, he had an OBE and

traveled to the shade of the oaks on the corner across from the menacing old house. There, he watched the sun rise in the window glass. His ethereal form had never yet known blue sky. It was beautiful, vibrant, with an eerie sense of expectation. The sun was almost fully risen when he heard, from deeper in the shadow of the oaks, a voice say, "I see you." Owen leaped out of sleep. The voice sounded like it was only two inches behind him. He'd felt the breath of the words against the back of his neck. He knew it wasn't a dream.

It was a brown suit, white shirt, no tie day. He was exhausted. Luckily, it was quiet at the library. There were whole half-hour patches through the morning when he could lean back in his office chair and nod off. Most who came in knew what they wanted and were gone in minutes. Though there was a young woman who scoured the children's section. Rubbing his eyes, a little annoyed by her presence, Owen got up and went to see if he could help her find what she was looking for. When he drew closer to the woman, he realized he knew her. It took him a second to place her as she stood and greeted him, and he reciprocated. The final clue was her red hair—it was Shiela Tobac.

"I'm looking for a certain reference book for the project I'm working on," she said.

Owen said, "Interesting," but left it at that.

"The book is titled *The Daily Reader*. It's a children's book."

"I know it," said Owen. "Stay here for a minute. Let me get it." He strode into the back room next to his office where the small book hospital was, along with a table stacked with new books to be processed for circulation. He went to the trash bin in the corner and dug down. His hands went directly to it. *The Daily Reader* rose again like a silver mummy. He brought it to her. "You can keep it," he said.

"Seriously?"

"Keep it," he said. "Otherwise, it's heading for the chopper."

She thanked him profusely and was gone in a minute. As he headed back to the office, he wondered if Shiela Tobac was subsuming other works of fiction into the ever-increasing, downhill-rolling snowball of her massive story. Immediately upon contact with his chair, he fell into a deep sleep—no traveling, no dreams, just pure oblivion. A solid hour passed without the bell attached to the front door going off. When he woke, he rose to consciousness slowly, like a diver trying to avoid the bends. There was the brutal pressure of so much to deal with in the waking world—monsters and schemes of assassination.

He stood and stretched his arms out, yawning. It was

so quiet away from town, near the woods, and no patrons, that he heard a car pull over to the curb out on
the street. He left his office to see who was visiting. Although she'd already been in once, he wouldn't mind seeing Shiela Tobac again. There was something about her
mad energy he found enchanting. The car by the curb
was a '70s Buick Skylark, metallic green, like something
from his father's era. He couldn't imagine Shiela Tobac
driving anything so stodgy. The door opened on the dri-
ver's side, the side away from the library, and out stepped
a man. He was a little stooped, with a bald head save for a
ring of white hair. Owen knew it was Crenshaw.

A vision of his own mutilated corpse, thorax split open
and leaking blood all over the children's section haunted
his thoughts. "Shit," he whispered, and bolted before the
old man could look up and see him through the glass
door. Owen could taste the adrenaline. His legs felt as
weak as in a dream, and his mouth had gone perfectly
dry. All he could hear was the sound of his own heartbeat. He made it to the counter and ducked behind it just
before he heard the door alarm in his office. The Ambrogio was in the library.

"Mr. Hapstead," the old man called. "Mr. Owen Hapstead! I've come to return the favor of last night." The
voice sounded to be coming from the children's section.
"Mr. Hapstead, meet me tonight in dreamland, why don't

you?"

There was silence, and Owen had to cover his mouth, as he knew he was breathing too desperately.

"My Sleeping Beauty," came the chilling voice. "It's disappearing, as perhaps you might soon as well."

Owen got on his hands and knees and crawled as fast as he could back through his office, down the short hallway, directly to the back door of the library. He slowly stood up and remained motionless. Crenshaw was banging on the bell at the counter. "Service, my good man," he yelled. "Service." He went on a tirade on the bell, banging it mercilessly, and when that storm of noise was at its most intense, Owen opened the door, which squealed more than he'd have liked, and bolted across the field of weeds toward the woods. It was the fastest he'd ever run, powered by sheer terror. When he reached the cover of the trees, he realized he'd left the pistol in the desk drawer of his office.

He ducked behind a tree and gathered himself into a ball with his arms around his knees. From behind him he heard the back door of the library squeal open. At this point, he was stunned and couldn't bring himself to look.

"See you tonight," called the voice across the field. A brief spell later, he heard the door close with a bang. And a few moments after, the old Buick out front started up and pulled away from the curb. Owen waited a good half hour before he ventured into the library. The back door locked on its own, so he had to go around the front. He was afraid the old man had only moved the car a way down the street to then return to ambush him. Eventually, it was clear he was gone for good, although Owen's fear of him pouncing never diminished.

In his office, on his desk, Owen found a painting, 10×13, done in a reddish-brown color. It took him a minute to process what he was looking at. At the same time, he realized the piece was a portrait of him and Melody in the night world, Crenshaw cutting their silver cords with his monstrous incisors. It had surely been executed in that poor fellow's blood who was suffering his last on the gurney on the third floor of the old man's house. The gore had not completely dried in one small patch, and the canvas stank like death. He lifted the painting with a pen shoved under the back of the frame and walked it directly outside to the dumpster behind the library, lifted the lid, and let it and the pen drop in. On his walk back to the front door, he allowed himself to stop breathing through his mouth.

15

KIARA AGAIN DROPPED WILLIAM off at Mrs. Hultz's place. The story this time was that she was just starting at a night job and she needed someone to watch William for a couple of shifts until a sitter from an agency was due to start. After she left her son, she went next door to Owen's. She didn't knock but just pushed open the door and walked in. He was in the kitchen, waiting. On the table in front of him were the pistol and a cup of coffee. He got up and poured her a cup. "You want anything in it?" he asked. She shook her head and sat down across from him.

"I've got news," said Owen. "He's coming for us in the night world tonight. He was at the library today to stoke my fears."

She smiled. "Which means he's going to be sleeping somewhere. I've got the flamethrower in my car. I've also got a new pistol, fully loaded with phosphorous rounds from a member of the solar cross. He drove down from New York last night."

"So, we'll try to keep the painter busy in the night world while you find and fry him."

She nodded. "You two don't have much protection against him."

"I don't know. Melody has hinted at a way of gaining physical advantage for a few moments. Not sure what she meant, but she's a real adept. She comes to the night world with an entire philosophy and code of ethics passed down from earlier generations. She's something special."

"Well, I hope she's good at running, too," said Kiara.

"By now, we're both good at that."

She told him how she and William had been on the run for the last couple of days, unable to go back to their apartment. Before leaving, at the door, she said, "I'll try to get him fast."

"It would be greatly appreciated."

He paced back and forth across the living room, impatient for sundown and the weary feeling, before he gave in for the night and went to bed. Eventually, he cautioned himself that he'd have to relax if he was going to get to sleep. Practicing the deep diaphragm breathing technique he'd learned in a college yoga class and hadn't used since, he sat in the corner of the couch with the light off and the TV quietly playing some black-and-white tearjerker from the '40s. He pushed out the thoughts of Crenshaw with the realization that his current life between home and the library had grown stale. He used the time behind his closed eyes, amid the purposeful breathing, to sort out where he wanted to be in a few more years. It struck him for the first time that his existence was like something out of an ill-conceived afterlife. He followed his own arguments here and there and so deeply, he woke to the night world, standing up in his phantom form from the couch.

He yawned and walked through his front door and out onto the street. It was a soft, beautiful night of stars. Still, the breeze insisted. He felt a great sense of anxiety in it, as if everything was aware something was about to happen. Melody stood on the corner beneath the streetlamp, her arms folded. She appeared deep in thought as he approached her. She looked up and smiled, and he said, "I have a question for you."

"OK."

"How did you know my phone number the other night to call and warn me about Kiara being trapped?"

"I always thoroughly research the lives of those I choose to mentor."

The fact that she must know quite a bit about his waking life embarrassed him, but he accepted her explanation. She had taught him a lot.

"I was here for a while," she told him as they walked along. "Scouting out some good spots for our encounter."

"Don't we have to head to the old man's house?"

"No," said Melody, "he'll find us. Let the monster do

the work. I say we head for the cemetery."

"Are you sure he'll come for us?"

She nodded.

"Why the cemetery?"

"Because at the very southern part of the place, moving to the north, is a miasma hungry and crackling for a sleeper."

"Poetic," he said.

"We're not just going to kill him; we're going to obliterate him from history. The night world is not without its element of irony," she said, and bounded into the starry sky in the direction of the cemetery. Owen followed and, at the height of his leaps, practiced midair somersaults. As they went along, he told her about Kiara's plans to barbecue the monster in his sleep.

"Kiara sounds fearless," said Melody.

"She's afraid the Ambrogio will eventually go after her son."

"She's right."

In minutes, they were passing the baseball diamond on the way to the cemetery. They both leaped at the same time, and at the apex of their ascent, Melody pointed toward the edge of the boundary of graves in the distance. Owen saw the miasma, the color of canary feathers, roiling just above the ground, and he could barely hear it sparking and whining. "I want to trap him in that," she said as they floated back to the ground. He wasn't sure her plan was sound. The Ambrogio had the upper hand, as he could separate them from their cords. They had each other and they had Melody's knowledge. But he thought messing with the miasma was cosmically wrongheaded. Owen considered that if by chance he was disintegrated—an utterly painful process he wasn't inclined to experience—in the morning, he would never have existed and there would be somebody else worrying about the rotting Sleeping Beauty at the library.

Once in the graveyard, Melody told him to get down behind one of the larger headstones and hide. They found two situated close by and both ducked. Owen kept looking nervously over his shoulder at the creeping yellow fog that was still a considerable distance away.

"So," he asked, "what am I supposed to do?"

"Don't let Crenshaw get too close to you. Remember, he can't grab you, but if he gets close enough, he can insert his hand into your chest and unhook your cord. Meanwhile, the ability you have over him is that you can jump up and put a good amount of distance between you and him in one bound."

"What am I supposed to do, then, ask him to walk into the miasma?"

"I think we should jump around him and confuse and

frustrate him as death draws closer. Then I will employ my maneuver, grab him—it only lasts a heartbeat or two—and throw him into oblivion."

"That sounds kind of iffy. Do you remember how fast and powerful he was when he went after Feit?"

"I'll use his ferocity against him and merely direct his energy as I've been taught."

Owen shook his head. "Sounds sketchy."

"My first teacher, Arthur Bishop, taught me how to deal with hostile entities."

"And during the day, you're just a mild-mannered mother and wife?"

"There's nothing mild-mannered about my approach to either of those," she said. "And I'm an insurance agent in addition to everything else."

"An insurance agent?" Owen laughed out loud. "You've been life insurance for me."

Melody nodded and smiled. "That's my specialty, life insurance. And I'm aware you're a librarian."

"Not fair. You know more about me than I do about you."

"I understand your library is going to disappear in a couple of years."

"Yeah," he said.

"Dedicate yourself to making it the best it can be in that short time?"

"That wasn't exactly my plan."

"What was your plan?"

"Sit and stare like a deer in the headlights until I'm either fired or transferred to the main branch."

"That's a plan for a blank-gaze cord-cutter. Seriously, what would be the difference? Life is passing you by."

He had a witty comeback, but it never got out as a voice drifted past them on the breeze. Instantly, he froze, knowing it was Crenshaw. "I smell fear," it said. Owen quickly looked over his shoulder to see how far off the miasma was, and then he peered around the headstone and saw the Ambrogio glowing a pale green, lunging forward in a crouch, ready to pounce. He looked over to Melody to see if she was watching. Unlike him, she'd stood straight up and was walking out from her hiding spot. "Keep moving," she whispered down to Owen, who was leaden with fright.

The next sound from Crenshaw was a growl. Anxiety built in Owen's chest and finally exploded. He sprang into the night sky. Below him he saw a pale green form pass through the headstone he'd been hiding behind. He looked quickly for Melody's location and saw her darting toward the miasma, drawing her target in. He floated down and nearly landed when he noticed the monster had reversed direction and was heading for him. Barely able to place his feet and leap, he darted up before the old man's fingers could pierce his phantom chest. Even under such duress, the absurdity of the night world never completely escaped him. Still, the proximity sent a bolt of terror shooting down his spine.

He lost sight of the Ambrogio for an instant, and that uncertainty, once he landed, made him spring immediately and recklessly in the direction he surmised Melody was. He immediately realized his mistake and looked up to see the miasma looming in front of him. His mind was overtaken by the memory of the fellow who'd leapt to his destruction from the roof of that house. Below he saw Melody dashing in front of and away from Crenshaw. Owen descended and could feel the heat and the crackling of the night air from the yellow mist. It sent out a feeler that snapped close to his left ear but missed. When he touched down again, the miasma reached for him with swirling wisps of fog, but he pushed off backward at a low trajectory and escaped, only to find himself passing through the pale green form of his attacker. There was a dark, frozen anguish at the center of his being. Landing, he launched himself up and away again.

The creature turned his attention to Melody, strategically trapping her between himself and the advancing fog on a plot of ground with open graves on either side. Owen yelled for her to jump, but she stood her ground. Crenshaw moved cautiously in as the miasma moved to within mere feet behind her. The old man's hand shot out toward her chest. Owen yelled to her again. In a flash, she somehow grabbed the Ambrogio by the forearms. There was a sudden look of consternation on the pale green face. He couldn't believe that her grasp and force had agency over him. She shifted her position as if she were about to throw Crenshaw into the mist. What she failed to notice was the clawed phantom hand coming up from under her arms.

As he witnessed the scene with a sense of horror, Owen heard a phone ring. The sound startled him, and he realized it was his phone. It looked like Melody had control of the beast but it also had her. His body vibrated throughout and he was brutally snatched back to himself. He woke in bed, shivering. The phone continued to ring, and he remained stunned. When he answered, he recognized Kiara's voice.

"Sorry to intrude, but I can't find the artist's body anywhere. Everything else is still here in this creepy-ass house—the blood vats, the hanging dried-out corpses."

"He's there," said Owen. "Somewhere. I know, 'cause Melody is right now wrestling him to the death."

"I'll go through the place one more time," she said.

"Where are you now?"

"Could be the living room."

The words "living room" set something off in Owen's

memory. He said, "Look up, over the couch. What do you see?"

"A big painting." There was a long silence.

"You see, in the picture, there's a chamber underneath the statue, and that statue is out back of the house. I ran into it the other night."

"Oh, shit, I see it," she said.

He heard her footsteps through the phone as she sped through the place. The entrance in the back of the house obviously had a screen door with a strong spring, as he heard the aluminum frame snap back and bang closed. The sound of Kiara breathing heavily followed.

"Look behind the statue," Owen called out, but it was clear she couldn't hear him. There were a few seconds of scuffling and muffled cursing before he heard her say "Yes" in a definitive tone. Next came her steps upon the concrete stairway, leading down. There was a gasp from Kiara and then that same growl he heard just minutes earlier in the cemetery. Two shots rang out and their sound made his phone vibrate. The growling came more fiercely, and then the whoosh of what he took to be the flamethrower. There was screaming.

Owen hung up. He sat in shock and his thoughts returned to Melody. He told himself he should try to go back to sleep and go to her aid in the night world. He lay back down and closed his eyes. It wasn't long before the phone rang again. He answered.

"He's finished," said Kiara. "The flames and the phosphorous bullets melted him. Once I was down in his lair, I didn't give him a chance."

Epilogue

OWEN DISCOVERED OVER THE next week that whatever automatic passage he'd had to the night world was gone. His struggles against sleep paralysis vanished, and instead, he had long, involved dreams of meeting Melody at different places in town. Every incident was rushed and full of insoluble complexities. Every morning, he woke with a sense of dread. And then five days later, he saw her obituary in the *Westwend Tattler*. "Died peacefully in her sleep. Survived by a son, a daughter, a husband." For the most part, he knew her only as a phantom, but he had seen her and her family in the grocery, and he mourned for their loss and his. On the same day, Kiara came to the library in the afternoon with William. She brought coffee for them and they sat on the bench out front while the boy played with a toy truck on the front path.

"Are you leaving?" he asked.

She nodded. "Going north to take a rest; the organization has given me a year off. My husband and I had been trying to bring Crenshaw down for a while and had lost a number of people, including Duane. They know they owe it to me."

"I'm glad I could help . . . if I did." Then he told her about Melody and they sat in silence for a brief time. As Kiara got up to leave, he told her about when he'd seen Melody in the market and what she and her family looked like in life. They both fell silent for a time, and then she gathered up William. At the car, Kiara put the child in his car seat. She beeped as she pulled away, and Owen waved.

A few months later, he sold his parents' house and bought a small ranch farther back in the barrens. The new location put an extra half hour on his walk to work. He returned to his route past the Busy Bee, though he never again entered the store. With the money left over after the purchase of the smaller house, he invested five thousand dollars in having the painting of Sleeping Beauty restored to its original look. The library was still slated to move and the building would be demolished. But there were still two years. The night of the day he called the restoration artists, he woke in his bed to a state of paralysis. Once again, he achieved the night world and wound up in the attic room of Shiela Tobac.

The red-haired girl was asleep on the cot in the corner, her glasses half on, a pencil between her fingers, and even though he didn't have to tiptoe to not be heard, he did.

He moved around the walls, lighting them just enough with his pale blue glow to see. Through voluminous chapters he searched, literally high and low, and discovered somewhere just above the baseboard, in the middle of the western wall, a mention of Melody.

He followed her story, which blew like a breeze through the otherwise greater plot of the novel. When he lost sight of it on one wall, he found it on another. The pieces came together like a puzzle the further he read. And then she was there, standing before chapter eleven, pale blue and beckoning him with open arms. He took a step toward her and caught only a brief glimpse of the dull center of her lifeless stare. She lunged and he woke. That was his last journey to the night world. For the rest of his life, he had to suffice with dreams.

Acknowledgments

Thanks to Ruoxi Chen and Irene Gallo at Tor.com Publishing for making this book possible. Also, a big thanks to John Klima, who let me interview him about what he does all day as a librarian besides hide in the stacks. And, of course, thanks to my agent, Howard Morhaim.

About the Author

Author photograph © Lynn Gallagher-Ford

Jeffrey Ford is the author of the novels *The Physiognomy, Memoranda, The Beyond, The Portrait of Mrs. Charbuque, The Girl in the Glass, The Cosmology of the Wider World,* and *The Shadow Year.* His story collections are *The Fantasy Writer's Assistant, The Empire of Ice Cream, The Drowned Life,* and *Crackpot Palace.* His short fiction has appeared in numerous journals, magazines and anthologies, from *MAD Magazine* to *The Oxford Book of American Short Stories.*

TOR·COM

Science fiction. Fantasy. The universe.

And related subjects.

*

More than just a publisher's website, *Tor.com*
is a venue for **original fiction, comics,** and
discussion of the entire field of SF and fantasy,
in all media and from all sources. Visit our site
today—and join the conversation yourself.